'What are y
doing?'

'I'm repaying the compliment,' he answered, an enigmatic little smile playing round his lips. 'Now I am staring at *you*.'

Saying no more, Eduardo freed her wrists, then started to unbutton the shapeless red white and blue patterned cardigan she wore.

'Now what are you doing?' she asked nervously, the touch of his strong muscled thighs in the tough denim of his jeans all but *burning* her skin through the slightly flimsier material of her own.

'I have a question for you.'

He locked his arms round her waist and Marianne stared up at him as if in a dream, yet fully and shockingly aware of the barely civilised, almost *feral* state of arousal reflected back at her from his haunting blue eyes. It was all she could do to keep breathing, never mind answer him.

'If I asked you to come to me tonight and share my bed...would you?'

The day **Maggie Cox** saw the film version of *Wuthering Heights*, with a beautiful Merle Oberon and a very handsome Laurence Olivier, was the day she became hooked on romance. From that day onwards she spent a lot of time dreaming up her own romances, secretly hoping that one day she might become published and get paid for doing what she loves most! Now that her dream is being realised, she wakes up every morning and counts her blessings. She is married to a gorgeous man, and is the mother of two wonderful sons. Her two other great passions in life—besides her family and reading/writing—are music and films.

BRAZILIAN BOSS, VIRGIN HOUSEKEEPER

BY

MAGGIE COX

All the characters in this book have no existence outside the imagination of the author, and have no relation whatsoever to anyone bearing the same name or names. They are not even distantly inspired by any individual known or unknown to the author, and all the incidents are pure invention.

First published in Great Britain 2009
Paperback edition 2010
Harlequin Mills & Boon Limited,
Eton House, 18-24 Paradise Road, Richmond, Surrey TW9 1SR

ISBN: 978 0 263 87769 4

Set in Times Roman 10½ on 13 pt
01-0210-43381

Harlequin Mills & Boon policy is to use papers that are natural, renewable and recyclable products and made from wood grown in sustainable forests. The logging and manufacturing process conform to the legal environmental regulations of the country of origin.

Printed and bound in Spain
by Litografia Rosés, S.A., Barcelona

BRAZILIAN BOSS, VIRGIN HOUSEKEEPER

To my fellow romance authors and readers
of romance everywhere—may we continue
to hold out for love, hope and happy endings
in these turbulent times, come what may!

CHAPTER ONE

NOTHING deterred her, it seemed. Not even weather that felt as if it was blowing in straight from Siberia, Eduardo mused. For the past three weeks he had taken to visiting the small historic market town more frequently than when he had first moved to the area—ostensibly drawn to a certain exhibition that had been running in the town hall—and he hadn't been able to help noticing the girl strumming her guitar at the side of the road, singing mournful folk songs and looking like some pretty waif straight out of a Dickens novel. Didn't she have parents, or people that cared about her? Apparently *not*…

It frankly appalled Eduardo that she was reduced to singing for her supper on the streets instead of earning her living by more comfortable means. It dawned on him that she was the first person to stir him out of his solitary existence for months—a state that had begun even before he had set foot on British shores from Brazil and made the impulsive decision to reside there. Well…the turbulent events of the past two years might have taken their toll, resulting in him becoming somewhat reclusive and distant from the rest of the human race, but he was definitely not looking for remedies to rectify that situation, he reminded himself. No… His interest in the girl was just a passing curiosity that would no doubt quickly fade. At any time she could move on, and he would likely never see her again. He paused to put a note into the tatty tweed cap that lay on the ground at her feet, and weighted it down with two fifty pence pieces to keep it from being snatched away by the wind.

'That's a pretty song,' he murmured.

'Thanks…but that's far too much.'

She stopped strumming and reached for the note, pressing it back into Eduardo's gloved hand. Their glances caught and held, and he had the most disturbing sensation that the ground had somehow shifted beneath him.

'Too much?' He raised a bemused eyebrow, certain he'd misheard her.

'Yes. If you want to donate some money to a charity there's a church just up the road, collecting for the local homeless…St Mary's. I'm neither a charity *nor* homeless.'

'But you have a hat with coins in it. Is that not why you stand here singing?'

A great irritation surfaced inside Eduardo, and he could hardly fathom the reason for the intensity of it—other than that he wasn't used to having his generosity rejected. *Why was he even wasting time talking to such a strange girl?* He should simply walk away, abandon her to her peculiar philosophy of singing for mere pennies and leave her be. But he found he could not. Even though the waif had insisted she was neither in need of charity nor a home, somehow her predicament had got to him—reached past his usual iron-clad defences and caused a surprising dent. It was—as he had concluded earlier—just that this was the first time for months that he had voluntarily made contact on purpose with someone else, and he hardly welcomed his considerate action being thrown back in his face.

'I sing because I'm compelled to…not for the money. Haven't you ever done something just for the sheer love of it and for no other reason?'

Her question struck him silent for a moment, and he barely knew what to do with the discomfort that made his skin prickle and burn and his throat lock tight.

'I—I have to go.'

Knowing his expression had become frozen and uncommunicative, as was his usual habit, Eduardo shrugged, suddenly eager to return to the anonymity of the rest of the passersby and the ponderous but familiar burden of his own tormented thoughts.

'Please yourself. You're the one that stopped to talk to me—remember?'

'I did not deliberately stop for the purposes of talking to you!' he flashed, his temper suddenly ignited by the girl's unflinching hazel gaze.

'I see that now. You merely wanted to make yourself

feel good by leaving me a ridiculously generous amount of money, then walk away again satisfied that you'd done your good deed for the day. Is that it?'

'You are impossible!'

Wishing with all his heart that he had ignored that bothersome rogue impulse to reach out to someone who he'd genuinely believed to be in need, Eduardo gripped the ivory handle of his walking cane and moved awkwardly away. He had practically reached the end of the street before his acute hearing once again picked up the strumming of the girl's guitar, along with her mournfully toned voice.

Had she been watching him? It troubled him deeply to realise that she must have been doing exactly that—else why wait so long to resume singing? Yes, she *had* been watching him…watching him walk away like the cripple he now was, he reflected savagely. Was she by any chance feeling sorry for him? The thought was like corrosive acid in his blood. Well, if he was ever unlucky enough to see her again he would make a deliberate point of ignoring her, he vowed. Who the hell did she think she was anyway—rebuffing his goodwill like that…*mocking* him, almost?

But as Eduardo painfully forced his stride into a more rapid pace, the question she'd asked echoed tauntingly round his brain and constricted his already tortured heart without mercy. *Haven't you ever done something just for the sheer love of it and for no other reason?* To his profound shame, moisture stung the back of his eyelids and, murmuring a vehement curse, he walked blindly on into the centre of town, hardly caring that his injured leg was taking unfair punishment—all because an insignificant slip of a girl had scorned his money and pricked his pride…

The temperature had plummeted to near freezing. Barely able to feel any sensation at all in her numbed fingers as they moved over the guitar strings, Marianne decided to call it a day. The idea of a mug of creamy hot chocolate nursed in front of a roaring fire drew her swiftly homewards, and she strove hard to blot out the fact that she would be returning to an empty house. A silent, echoing mausoleum, where everything from the daintiest ornament to the lovely music room with its shining grand piano was a haunting reminder of the husband and friend who had been taken from her much too soon…

'Move on with your life when I'm gone,' Donal had feverishly entreated her from his hospital bed, with a light burning in his eyes that had scared Marianne, because it had told her that he wouldn't hang on for much longer. 'Sell the damn house and everything in it, if you want! Go and see the world…meet new people, travel…*live*, for God's sake. Live for the both of us.'

And she would…but not yet. She was still finding her bearings without a compass, in a world empty of the one person who had really cared for her. She was inching forward slowly but surely.

Busking in the street might seem a strange place to start. But having had a dread of performing in public that she wanted to overcome, so that from time to time she could sing in the local folk club without going to pieces, as far as moving on with her life went Marianne saw it as an entirely positive step. Not only was she facing down her fear and thriving at the same time, she was saying to the universe *Is that the worst you can do? Take my husband from me and leave me alone again? Well, just watch this!* Every day she was becoming more and more confident. Yet again, music had saved her. Donal would have been proud that she'd found the courage to take such a radical if *unconventional* step towards her own healing—even if his two adult children from his previous marriage were *not*, instead taking it as a sign that she must be unstable… A sign that she must have had some 'not quite right' influence on their father, to make him ignore them and leave everything to her in his will instead.

Just then, out of the blue, a stranger's chiselled hard face overlaid her husband's kind, familiar one, and Marianne was shocked to recall the man who had put a fifty-pound note in her cap. Not for one second did she doubt it had been the real deal. Not only had he looked wealthy—as if he lived an elite lifestyle that was way beyond the ordinary dreams of a secure, comfortable life for regular people—but he had *smelled* wealthy too. He'd spoken perfect English, with a trace of an accent—South American, perhaps? He had also exuded the kind of authority that would have made Marianne shrink inside herself not so very long ago. But nursing Donal through his long, ultimately fatal illness, then sitting beside his hospital bed for nigh on two months while he clung doggedly to life before lapsing into a coma, had fostered in her the type of courage and tenacity that she was determined never to be without again.

Cupping her mug of hot chocolate, she stared into the crackling flames in the fireplace, the compelling features of the man who had disturbed her becoming even stronger in her mind. Marianne had never seen eyes quite that unique shade of blue before. They'd been the frosted hue of a cloudless winter sky and, although his hair had had tones of amber-gold threaded through its tawny strands, his lashes had been the intense dark brown of richly melting chocolate. He'd had an aquiline nose, with a slight bump in the bridge and his mouth, though firm and well-shaped, had nonetheless been so stern that it had seemed to suggest it would physically pain him to smile. Even though she had briefly conversed with him, she still got the impression that he projected the kind of impenetrable fortress that even a seasoned campaigner didn't have a hope of breaching! After she had declared she didn't sing just for money, challenging him with her question as to if he hadn't ever done something just for the sheer love of it, Marianne had immediately regretted her outburst.

She squirmed at the ill-mannered way she had accused him of trying to make himself feel good by putting so much money in the hat. She shouldn't have done that. How could *he* know that after the tragedy she had suffered she'd vowed never to accept or need help from anybody ever again? That her trust in anything good had been utterly shattered when, after a hellish childhood with a neglectful alcoholic father, she'd finally found some happiness in her marriage, only for her husband to die just six months later?

But the stranger had stared back at her as if he'd had his own demons to face, she remembered, and for a few tense moments there Marianne had barely known what to think or do as she met his stricken gaze. Then, before she'd had a chance to apologise, he had walked away… *limping*. Had he suffered an accident or been ill? It didn't seem right that such a big, well-made and relatively *young* man should have such an obvious infirmity—though it didn't lessen the impact of his imposing stature and riveting carved features at all…merely *added* to those assets.

Frowning, Marianne realised she had watched him almost as though in a trance…as if totally forgetting where she was or what she was doing. Then the biting cold that had been like the touch of knives against her face had forced her attention back to the present, and she'd resumed her playing and singing with a stoic determination to defy the worst the weather could throw at her. But underneath her singing Marianne had been completely bemused, and not a little shocked that a total stranger could command her attention so avidly….

* * *

'You've been overdoing it again, haven't you?'

'For God's sake, I'm not a child!' Grimacing at the older man's frowning face, Eduardo wished he could dispense with the doctor's fortnightly visits for good. But after nine operations on his shattered leg he had needed access to regular medical attention once settling in the UK, and Evan Powell was one of the top orthopaedic surgeons in Harley Street. Plus, he had been recommended to him by his own surgeon back in Rio de Janeiro.

'Then take my advice, man, and stop treating your body as though it were some mechanical machine instead of very human flesh and bone!'

'I was told I would recover complete and normal use of my leg, given time,' the younger man challenged impatiently. 'Why the hell is it taking so long?'

'Your femur was all but crushed in the accident. The bone has been practically rebuilt from scratch. Did you really expect to recover from nine major operations as easily as you would get over a cold?'

'When I want your opinion on how I conduct myself,' Eduardo hissed, his already sour mood worsening by the second, 'I will ask for it!'

'Well, then…' Powell retrieved his cashmere coat from the winged-back chair to fold it carefully over his arm. As tidily as he no doubt expected his staff to lay out the surgical instruments of his profession in theatre before an operation, Eduardo mused without humour. 'Don't bother calling your man. I'll see myself out and bid you goodnight, Mr De Souza.'

'It's been a bad day—' he started, rising to his feet from his chair, bitterly suppressing a groan of pain after the short but thorough examination of his leg by the surgeon. Eduardo glanced at the ornate French antique clock on the marble mantelpiece. Sometimes he marveled that time continued as it did on its relentless course, when the tragedy that had ripped his wife and her unborn child away and all but left him a useless cripple should by rights have stopped the world in its tracks. 'I should not have spoken to you like that. It was good of you to come out all this way on such an inclement night as this. Forgive me.'

'No harm done.'

Quickly overcoming any offence he might have taken previously, Evan Powell shrugged his rather bony shoulders in his charcoal-grey pin-striped suit, then glanced interestedly round the beautiful lamp-lit drawing room, with its huge bay windows overlooking the surrounding moat, a network of fields and the dense forest beyond it. A landscape that was now shrouded in the blanket of surely one of the most severe winter frosts on record.

'Perhaps what you need is some company?' he suggested, the sudden 'man to man' glint in his eye speaking volumes. 'You're very isolated out here, and it would help to take your mind off things'

Eduardo's gaze narrowed. 'You mean a woman?' What surprised him was that for the first time in two years he didn't immediately dismiss the idea. What *shocked* him was that in response to this suggestion his mind helpfully conjured up for him a very engaging picture of the roadside busker, with her big hazel eyes, pretty mouth and rippling river of honey-brown hair. He was suddenly appalled at himself. How old was she? Seventeen…eighteen? Had good common sense deserted him along with everything else that mattered? He might indeed be ready for some female company *recreationally*, but in no other respect did he wish to be close to a woman.

After what had happened to Eliana he was done with relationships for good.

When he did not immediately answer the other man, the surgeon shrugged again, the edges of his thin-lipped mouth lifting in a conciliatory smile. 'Just a suggestion, dear fellow… Now, listen to my advice and take it easy on that leg. I recommend just a twenty-minute walk each day—half an hour if you must, but no more than that. In the meantime, if you want to talk about any aspect of your recuperation, I've let my secretary know that I will accept your calls at any time so long as I'm not in the operating theatre. I'll see you next time. Goodnight.'

Almost as if intuiting that his employer's visitor was about to depart, Eduardo's valet Ricardo appeared in the doorway, the spots of damp across his jacket's dark shoulders suggesting he'd already been hard at work outside, clearing some of the ice from the long sweeping drive that led away from the house.

'Goodnight, Mr Powell…and thank you once again for coming out on such a night. Please drive safely.'

* * *

In the early hours of that same morning, Eduardo tried his hardest to concentrate on the 1940s black and white comedy playing on the flat state-of-the-art television screen in front of him. But even a scant moment of pleasure or comfort frustratingly eluded him. He had got into the habit of watching movies well into the small hours, simply because he could not settle his mind enough to sleep. *Not when it dwelled on one set of terrible events over and over again, like a nightmarish film stuck on rewind.* Some nights he couldn't face even going to his bedroom at all, so he simply pulled a rug over him on one of the comfortable leather sofas in the sitting room and dozed there till morning. Pain… burning and torturous…often shot through his injured leg and hip, adding to his woes.

Stoically ignoring the all too tempting urge to pour a glass of whisky to drown his sorrows and dull his pain, Eduardo muttered a passionate expletive. Rubbing at his increasingly tense brow as he attempted to watch the impossibly glamorous characters cavort on the screen before him, he quickly abandoned the whole idea and pressed the 'off' button on the remote. Even losing himself in distraction seemed impossible. It was as though he was permanently staring into a black abyss there was no escape from, and all hope of ever seeing daylight or sensing warmth again was lost to him for ever.

Releasing a bitter sigh, he reflected that even that pretty busker in the street was no doubt far happier with her simple hand-to-mouth existence than he could ever hope to be with his immensely wealthy and privileged one.

Why did he seem to be fixating on her? he wondered. Impatiently he shook his head. His interest made no sense—especially when she had spoken to him with the offhand brusqueness of inexperienced youth, making it more than clear that she obviously disdained his desire to help. But, nonetheless, time and time again in the too-long frosty night at his isolated house, Eduardo found his thoughts returning to the girl, wondering if she really did have a place to stay, if she had made enough money to eat that day, and if she was warm on this bitterest of winter nights?

By the time a reluctant grey dawn had seeped in between the parted velvet drapes the next morning he had more or less decided that the next time he ventured into town he would *not* ignore her, as he had previously vowed. No…instead he would talk to her, question her about her circumstances, and maybe offer to help better her situation. *Was he a complete fool for contemplating such a potentially disastrous course of action?* It was quite likely that she would laugh in his face or tell him to go and find some other poor down and out to foist his money on!

Finally, concluding that his desire to be of assistance was being prompted by the idea of his own child struggling in a similar situation, had he or she lived to be the age of this girl, he swallowed down the lump of anguish in his already tight throat and, making himself as comfortable as he was able on the couch, at last drifted off to sleep…

CHAPTER TWO

MARIANNE was between songs, sipping café latte from a local coffee shop to warm her up and hopefully restore some heat into her blood again, on yet another day chilly enough to turn solid stone into a block of ice. All of a sudden a shaft of pure, undiluted sunlight arrowed down onto the pavement a few yards in front of her, trapping in its beam a golden head that riveted her attention. *It was him!* The expensive-looking guy with the stern mouth and the ivory topped cane. He didn't seem to be limping as badly today, Marianne reflected, watching him, and her insides executed an unsettling somersault as she saw that he was definitely heading her way.

Moments later he stood before her, his breath making a little puff of frosted steam as he spoke. 'Good afternoon,' he said politely, and there was a barely discernible lift to one corner of that impossibly serious mouth that surprisingly might have been the beginning of a smile.

'Hello,' she murmured, her gloved hand tightening round her take-away coffee cup.

'You are not singing?'

'No…I'm taking a break. Warming myself up.'

Finding herself the target of his devastating silent scrutiny, Marianne felt her entire body tense with discomfort. *Did he have any idea how intently he stared?* His eyes were like twin frosted blue lasers, making an exploratory dive straight down into her soul. Her husband Donal had never regarded her in such an intense way. *His* gaze had simply been infinitely kind.

'How's business?'

'Okay.' Shrugging, Marianne glanced down at the small collection of coppers and silver change in the hat at her feet. 'Like I told you before, I don't sing just for—'

'Money. I remember. You sing because you are compelled to…for the love of it, yes?'

'Yes.' Now she felt embarrassed, remembering her outburst of the other day. 'Look, I'm sorry if I offended you in any way by what I said or did, but there are a lot of people far worse off than me you know? In fact I'm not badly off at all. Appearances can be deceiving.'

His tanned brow creased a little, as if he were silently disputing her assessment of her situation, and his gaze carefully took in her mismatched woollen clothing that today consisted of purple tights, brown boots, a red dress over a cream sweater and Donal's too-big sheepskin lined leather jacket, with a beige scarf tucked into the neckline to keep out the worst of the cold. The only thing she wasn't wearing to finish off the eye-catching ensemble was her multi-coloured ski hat. Rushing out of the house this morning, she had accidentally left it behind.

'Well...if it helps you to know, I did in fact donate the money I would have given you to the church's collection for the homeless, as you suggested. Let me introduce myself. My name is Eduardo De Souza.' Balancing one hand on his cane, he removed a glove and struck out his now bare hand towards her.

For what seemed like an interminable second of agonising decision-making Marianne hesitated, before slipping her own gloved hand lightly into his. Even through the thickly knit wool she swore she sensed the heat from his body radiate up her arm, making her tingle. 'I'm Marianne...Marianne Lockwood. You're clearly not from around here, are you?'

'I reside in the UK now, but I do not come from here...you are right. I am from Brazil...Rio de Janeiro.'

'The land of samba, sunshine and *carnaval*? I'm sorry—I expect you hate that cliché.'

'Not at all. I am proud of my country and what it has to offer.'

'And you'd rather be here, turning into a human ice-pole, than at home soaking up the sun?' She couldn't suppress the teasing grin that took hold of her lips, but Eduardo de Souza's grave expression did not lighten for a moment.

'Even sunshine can pall after a time, if you have too much of it. It becomes commonplace, and one can easily risk losing the pleasure that was once derived from it,' he commented seriously. 'Besides…I am half-British, so I am not completely unfamiliar with this climate—and after the winter comes the spring, and that is consoling, yes?'

'I know. I love the spring! So…what are you doing here today? Shopping? Meeting a friend?'

'Neither. I've been visiting an exhibition that is on at the town hall. Surprisingly, there are quite a few places of interest to visit in this quaint little town.'

'True. It gets quite packed in the summer, believe it or not.'

'I can believe it.'

Now, to Marianne's complete surprise, her companion *did* smile, and his eyes looked bright as stars for a moment. Something inside her reacted disturbingly strongly to the fact and she felt her skin tighten self-consciously.

'Yes there are boat trips you can take on the river, and they're always very popular with the tourists. Anyway…'

Coming to the end of her coffee, Marianne stood the empty cup on the pavement behind her, then picked up the guitar that lay in its open black case on the ground beside it. Surprised that such an urbane, clearly wealthy man as Eduardo de Souza would even bother to introduce himself to a girl like her—particularly in such *unusual* circumstances—she couldn't help but be cautious. But then, as she glanced at that movie-star-handsome face and the commanding physique the cashmere coat he wore hinted at, it seemed unlikely that his intent was anything other than to pass the time of day with her. Anything else would be preposterous. They'd had a bit of an exchange before, and he was merely being polite, she told herself.

'I'm sorry, but I'm going to have to get back to what I'm here for.' Removing her gloves, Marianne strummed a few chords to tune her guitar. A group of visiting French students passing by just then momentarily peered at her with interest. As for her handsome visitor, he stubbornly remained where he stood, apparently in no hurry to leave.

'Next time…when I am in town…perhaps you would allow me to buy you lunch?' he suggested.

Marianne blinked. Even the *idea* of sitting in some smart little restaurant opposite this man for an hour or more made her go hot and cold. For a start, what would they possibly have in common to talk about? 'Thank you, but no,' she answered quickly. 'I don't really do lunch when I'm working'

'You mean you do not take a break to eat?' He sounded amused.

'I do take a break, but only to have coffee and sometimes maybe a croissant or a muffin…I have my main meal in the evening…when I get home.'

'Then how about I buy you coffee and cake instead?'

No reason to refuse him coming helpfully to mind, Marianne nodded uncomfortably. 'Okay. Now, I really have to get back to this.'

'Then I will say goodbye, Marianne.' He briefly inclined his head, his expression inscrutable. 'Until next time.'

'Next time' turned out to be two days later. Having endured an icy shower of rain and sleet combined for the previous hour, huddled beneath an inadequate umbrella instead of playing her guitar, Marianne had seriously thought about packing up and calling it a day. But then the sun came out, the freezing cold shower subsided, and as if by magic Eduardo De Souza appeared. He was dressed in his stylish cashmere coat, with a matching scarf draped casually round his neck, and his attire seemed much more suitable for the premiere of a theatre production rather than a casual visit to town.

'Hello.' He smiled, his rich voice sounding a little huskier than she remembered. Realising that for the past two days she had subconsciously been looking out for him, her heart thudding with what felt ridiculously like excited anticipation whenever his image crossed her mind, Marianne struggled to make her response sound natural.

'Hi…' she mumbled, standing back to shake the drops from her umbrella, fold it, then lean it against the wall. 'Not exactly the *best* day for coming into town,' she quipped.

'Fortunately I missed the downpour. I have spent the past hour under cover at the exhibition.'

'The same exhibition you visited before?'

'Yes.'

'It must be quite compelling to make you want to visit it again. What's it about?'

'It's a collection by a French photographer I particularly admire…a retrospective of his life in Paris just after the war, when the city was being rebuilt. He died recently, and I saw an article in the local newspaper advertising the exhibition.'

'Oh.' Collecting her guitar from its case, Marianne gave her visitor an awkward smile. 'I should probably go and take a look at it myself before it ends. It sounds fascinating.'

'You are interested in the subject?'

'I'm always interested in creativity and art—whatever its form. It intrigues me to learn how other artists see the world…how they interpret what they see. Just goes to show we all see things so differently…not in the same way at all.'

For a moment the man in front of her fell silent, as though he were seriously considering the opinion Marianne had just expressed, and with no small amount of surprise either.

Then he glanced down at his watch—expensive-looking, but definitely not ostentatious. 'How about going for that coffee now?'

Again finding no immediate reason to decline, and feeling chilled to the bone after that hour of relentless sleet and rain, Marianne found herself agreeing. 'Okay. Now's as good a time as any, I suppose.'

* * *

In the familiar café, with its cheerful red and white checked curtains and matching tablecloths, the aromatic smell of brewing coffee mingling with the steam arising from the damp coats of customers gratefully seeking warmth, shelter and sustenance after their tussle with the elements, Marianne was mildly surprised to find it as busy as it was. Luckily she found a small table close to the woodstove, and the waitress appeared almost straight away to take their order. She didn't doubt it was because Eduardo did not look like your average everyday customer—his almost regal bearing and sheer physicality alone commanded instant attention.

Goodness knew what the poor girl made of Marianne as his companion! As it was, she saw her look slightly askance at her guitar in its battered case, as if it was something almost distasteful. Eduardo gave her their order, and Marianne suddenly found herself alone with him. Resting his hands atop the checked tablecloth, he studied her without speaking. *What was he thinking?* Marianne wondered nervously. She cleared her throat and forced a shaky smile, feeling ill at ease and somehow graceless in her jumble of ill-fitting clothing beneath his intense examination.

'This is a nice place. It makes a change from the local coffee chain I usually use. The coffee's very good, and the pastries aren't bad either.'

'I am glad you chose a table near the fire…you look half frozen!'

'I'm not any more. I'm quite warm, actually.' Undoing

several buttons on her coat, Marianne flashed him a smile, genuinely touched by the concern in his voice.

'I have to ask you—' the disturbing glance seemed to intensify '—are your parents happy about you singing at the side of the road?' he questioned, frowning.

She could tell by his tone that he disapproved.

'They're not around any more to have an opinion,' she answered instantly, without thinking, and then a splinter of indignant anger pierced her that he should disapprove of people he didn't even know. 'Anyway…I don't mean to be rude…it's really none of your business.'

'How old are you? Seventeen…eighteen?'

Marianne stopped fiddling with the sugar bowl on the table and stared at him with the hardest gaze she could muster. 'For your information, I'm twenty-four—and quite capable of looking after myself *and* making my own decisions without the interference or permission of *anyone* else, including parents if they were around!'

'It is just that you appear much younger…' Eduardo murmured, his returning gaze completely unapologetic.

'It's hardly my fault if genetics or fate has made me look younger than I am!'

'I am not criticising the way you look, Marianne.' His voice softened, and so did his gaze. 'I am just concerned that you would choose to put yourself in what could potentially be a very vulnerable position. Can you not find somewhere else…somewhere *safer* where you might perform your songs?'

'There's a folk club I sing at sometimes…but it's

only open once every fortnight. I'd get very rusty if that was my only outlet. Besides…' Fearing his judgement and disapproval, Marianne slotted her defences firmly into place. 'The vendors that work in the market look out for me. Someone immediately comes over if it looks like anyone is bothering me.'

Eduardo sighed. 'That at least makes me feel a little easier about the situation.'

'Well, please don't give it another thought. I've been singing outside for over a year now, and nothing dire has happened to me yet!'

The waitress brought their coffee, along with two generous slices of the fruitcake Eduardo had ordered for them. Marianne added sugar to her drink and stirred it.

His expression at her words revealed more alarm than reassurance, and her companion reached into his inside coat pocket for his wallet, extracted something, and held it out to her. Initially thinking he was going to offer her money, Marianne was about to give him short shrift when she thankfully saw that he was actually offering her a small business card.

'What's this for?'

'If you ever need anything…'

'What could I possibly need from a complete stranger?' For some inexplicable reason she found herself precariously close to tears. Some renegade emotion had crept up on her undetected, until it was almost too late to rein it in again. *It had been happening a lot lately.*

The Brazilian firmed his mouth. 'A job, for one

thing… And, seeing as we are sitting here together having coffee, I hope I am no longer a stranger. If this weather gets much colder—and the forecast is not good for the rest of January—you might appreciate an alternative way to earn some money. A job that would also provide a roof over your head and good, nourishing food to eat.'

'What kind of job?' Intrigued now, despite herself, Marianne glanced out of the window at the steel-grey sky and the threat of even more sleet and snow. An involuntary tremor went through her.

'I need a housekeeper.' The broad shoulders beneath the fawn-coloured cashmere lifted, then fell again.

'A housekeeper?'

'I already have a valet to do the personal things I need help with…but, having resided here for almost a year now, I find it has become increasingly clear that some extra help in the house would be most welcome. At present I hire contract cleaners, and Ricardo—my valet—does the cooking. But if you can cook too that would alleviate him of that particular task and no doubt be most welcome. Give it some thought and ring me if you would like to give it a try. The house is a little remote, but if you do not mind that and enjoy beautiful countryside views then I do not think you will be disappointed.'

'And you would give me this job without even knowing if I could do it?' Marianne's hazel eyes were sceptical.

'You seem a very independent sort of person to

me…the type who would learn quickly, get on with things and not make a fuss. I am sure you would work out just fine.'

'Are you normally so trusting of people you don't even know? I could be anyone! What if I pinched the silver, or some priceless family heirloom whilst under your roof?'

Astonishingly, both corners of Eduardo's severe mouth lifted at the same time. For a moment Marianne's breath caught at the flash of humour that transformed his compelling pale blue eyes.

'Would a girl who sings in the street for pennies and hands me back a fifty-pound note, telling me to give it to the homeless, be likely to steal even a crust of bread from her employer?' He shook his head, his expression reverting to seriousness again. 'I do not think so.'

'Well, I thank you for your concern, as well as the offer of a job, but I'm not ready for a change just yet. As long as there's not a full-blown blizzard then I'll continue to sing outside for the foreseeable future.'

'Very well… That is your decision, of course. Why don't you try your fruitcake? It looks very good.'

'Thank you. I will.'

The rest of their conversation was politely superficial and companionable—as though they had silently recognised the potential danger in discussing anything more personal and mutually agreed to avoid it.

Twenty minutes later they parted—Marianne to return to her singing, and Eduardo to head wherever he was heading. She hadn't asked him where. But as he moved away from her and continued on down the street her heart definitely raced a little as she watched him go. Remembering his surprising offer of a job, she wondered why she suddenly felt so bad for refusing his help. Was it because she thought she'd detected a hint of melancholy or sadness in that magnetising gaze as they'd sat talking? Was it anything to do with the reason he walked with a cane? A wave of sympathy tugged hard at her heartstrings.

'Sing us a song, love!' One of the cheerful vendors who sold fruit from a stall further down the street stopped in front of her, clapping his gloved hands together with an exaggerated shiver. 'We need something to warm us up. It's colder than bloody Siberia today, *and* there's heavy snow forecast for tonight. Got any songs about spring?'

Shaken out of her reverie, Marianne grinned. 'How about "By the Banks of the Sweet Primroses"?'

'Lovely job!' The vendor happily grinned back.

When the notion of trying to help the little roadside singer had come to him, it hadn't even crossed Eduardo's mind to offer her a job. So when the words had come out of his mouth he'd surprised even himself. Contract cleaners he could maintain an aloof distance from, and the familiar Ricardo whom he'd brought with him from Rio de Janeiro were one thing—but to invite a new young acquaintance to share his roof and become his housekeeper was quite another. Especially when he guarded his privacy more fiercely than Fort Knox was famed for guarding its gold bullion.

But it was perfectly true that he *did* need a housekeeper, and considering Marianne's shivering form yesterday, watching her struggle to keep warm in the bleak winter weather, Eduardo had suddenly thought it was the ideal solution. *But she had turned him down.* It was true that he had not really believed that she would accept his offer, but still…it *irked* him more than a little that she had not. And it was a practical certainty that if he attempted to offer her money again, to help better her situation, she would likely throw it back in his face and instruct him in no uncertain terms to go to hell! She had a temper on her, that was for sure. And it had genuinely shocked him to learn that she was no teenager but twenty-four years old…a *woman*.

Recalling the flash of fire in her almond-shaped hazel eyes as she'd castigated him for being too intrusive, he felt his skin tighten hotly. Irritably ignoring the unsettling sensation, he strode into the ornate marble bathroom that led off his private suite of rooms and for several moments just stood in the centre of the floor, unsure why he had even gone in there. Restlessly he pushed his fingers through his hair and sighed. It was probably best he curb his philanthropic urges where that particular young woman was concerned and concentrate his efforts on repairing his damaged leg, doubling his belief that one day soon he would be able to walk as well as he had before the accident—confidently, and without even a trace of a limp.

After that...Eduardo moved across to the vanity unit, staring at his reflection in the large oval mirror there and grimacing at the deep shadows wrought beneath his eyes by agony of body and spirit and a severe lack of sleep. *After that...* Well, he would just have to take one day at a time, he told himself, hardly able to contemplate a future that wasn't as bleak and pain-filled as the present. How could such a prospect be possible when the two lives most intimately intertwined with his had been ripped away? When every night he relived the terrible nightmare of the accident that had killed them—the accident that *he* had caused?

CHAPTER THREE

THERE was indeed a heavy snowfall that night, as the fruit vendor had predicted. After surveying the cloak of sparkling white that blanketed her garden as well as the street outside the next morning Marianne tidied the house, made herself a hot drink, then tinkered with an unfinished song she'd been composing on the piano. *But her mood was not buoyant, and she struggled to stave off the sense of melancholy that kept threatening to overwhelm her.* Finally, unable to bear the enforced isolation a moment longer, she donned a warm coat, boots and a hat over her jeans and sweater and went outside.

The ice in the air snatched at her breath, making her eyes water, but her spirits lifted at just being out in the open again. She took herself off for a long, if *laboured* walk, due to the impediment of snow, into the park nearby. Just watching the children toboggan down the glistening frosted hillside and hurl snowballs at each other restored her sense of perspective *and* her good humour. And if any thoughts of the childhood *she'd* experienced, which had been bereft of similar happy times and feeling secure started to threaten, she firmly pushed them away, knowing it was pointless to contemplate such things when her cheerful mood could so easily regress to one of despair.

By the time she returned home she'd made a vow to fight off any gloomy recollection that might seduce her into unwanted misery. She simply would not allow herself to go there. But by mid-afternoon, when early darkness had descended, impelling her to turn on all the lamps again and draw the curtains, Marianne was sitting in an armchair in front of the fireplace, watching the flames lick round the burning coals and crackling twigs, and considering the prospect of life on her own again for the foreseeable future. *Donal would be so mad at her for sitting here feeling sorry for herself! That was for sure.* And suddenly she was crying. An unstoppable flow of hurt and sadness long dammed up could no longer be contained—making her weep until she was utterly spent and could cry no more.

Taking herself off to bed, she curled up in a foetal position, drawing the duvet right over her head, feeling numbed and empty. Just before she closed her eyes she swore to herself she would never indulge in such futile self-pity again. Tomorrow was a new day, and when the morning light came it would herald a new and more positive beginning. Marianne was *adamant* about that.

However, on lifting a corner of the bedroom curtains the following morning and being confronted by an even thicker blanket of snow, with a fresh shimmering fall of delicate white descending before her very eyes, she had to draw on every ounce of resolve not to be downcast. During the night she had made her mind up about something, and today there was plenty to occupy her towards implementing that decision.

Donal's adult children—Michael and Victoria—had contested the will that he'd made, leaving his house and all his belongings to Marianne. For nearly eighteen months she'd endured formal, aloof and *cruel* letters from their solicitor, stating the reasons for their dispute and insinuating that both she *and* their father had not been of sound mind, and now she had had enough. *They could have the house and everything in it.* She would leave it to them without a backward glance or a single regret.

She was certain Donal would forgive her. Everything he'd done for her in helping to restore her low self-esteem and encouraging her to believe in her talents and abilities she totally appreciated, but the truth was Marianne did not want to be beholden to anyone any more. Not even her deceased husband. She needed to be free again…free to live her life the way *she* chose—*however* that looked to anyone else. So, from the house she would take just her clothing, her guitar, and what little savings she had put by. Everything else—even the gifts Donal had bought her during their short-lived marriage—she would leave to his avaricious children.

Galvanised into action, she spent the day cleaning the house, restoring stray books to shelves, packing up her things and moving furniture back to where it had been when she had first moved in with Donal. Her body throbbed with satisfying warmth from a job well done, and she was too physically tired to allow even *one* negative thought to invade her mind. And that night… that night she slept like a baby.

But when she woke the next morning to find that the snow still hadn't cleared, and with no prospect of getting into town to play her guitar and sing—knowing she would be mad even to try—Marianne impulsively found herself searching for the business card Eduardo de Souza had insisted she take. Lifting the telephone receiver in the hall, she dialled his home number with shaking fingers. Even as she dialled she called herself all kinds of fool for contemplating such a *reckless* path.

But she could be snowbound for days, she thought, genuine dread invading her as she waited for someone to pick up at the other end. And now that she'd made the decision to leave and forge a new life, a new future, she was *eager* to put the past behind her and start again. *Something* had to be done to help improve her situation besides overcoming her fear of performing in public and accepting that she was now on her own again. Unlikely as it seemed, this might, just *might*, be it.

'Hello?' an accented male voice answered.

'Is that Mr De Souza?' Marianne ventured, her heart beating like a military tattoo.

'No. May I ask who is calling?'

It must be his valet, she realised, and taking a deep breath she said clearly, 'Marianne Lockwood. Is he available to speak?'

After a pause the man replied, 'Wait a moment, please. I will see.'

There were several times after the man went to locate his employer that Marianne almost put the phone down. *What was she doing?* she asked herself. She didn't know the first thing about being a housekeeper, and neither did she know what kind of an employer Eduardo De Souza would turn out to be. No doubt he would be overly serious and exacting, finding constant fault should she fail to measure up, examining her with that intense stare of his and making her rue the day she'd made the impulsive decision to go and work for him.

Yet beneath the cacophony of doubt and apprehension that raged inside her, a stronger more positive instinct was urging Marianne to go for it and give it a try.

'Marianne?'

Her prospective employer's voice—impatient and a little out of breath, as if he'd been interrupted in the middle of something and resented it—sounded in her ear.

'Hello, there. It's Marianne—the busker from town,' she explained, a light tremor in her voice. 'I—I hope you don't mind me ringing, but you said…'

'What is it that you need?'

Marianne glanced up to the heavens for courage. 'A job…and a home,' she replied, then made herself breathe deeply and mentally count to ten, so that she didn't succumb to her fears and change her mind. 'Are you still looking for a housekeeper?'

Sweat broke out on Eduardo's brow. The visiting physiotherapist might have been a torturer straight out of the Spanish Inquisition, he thought grimly as the man manipulated his scar-criss-crossed leg into yet another excruciatingly painful position to test its flexibility. He swore…*loudly*. The therapist looked startled and carefully moved his patient's leg back down onto the treatment couch with a murmured apology. Staring up at the ornately plastered Victorian ceiling in the library as he lay there, Eduardo sensed his racing heart slowly return to a more normal rhythm.

'Are we finished?' he asked, gravel-voiced.

The sandy-haired physio gave him a respectful and sympathetic smile. 'I agree you've probably had enough for now, Mr De Souza. My advice is to take it easy for the rest of the day. Try and get some proper rest tonight, and don't overdo things.'

'Do they teach you at medical school to come out with these clichéd platitudes?' Eduardo remarked irritably, swinging his legs over the side of the table and ignoring the other man's immediate move to help him.

Unoffended, the man smiled again. 'Sometimes rest really *is* the best course of action when dealing with any kind of physical trauma,' he explained. 'The body needs to access its own powers of healing, and rest gives it the opportunity to do that. I realise it may have been a little uncomfortable for you today, but the fact is your leg *is* definitely recovering from that last operation. Another month or two and you should notice a significant improvement when walking. I can practically guarantee it.'

'Give me your hand,' Eduardo muttered, and accepted help to stand—though it psychologically pained him to accept *anyone's* help these days, when he had previously been so fit and able.

Hearing the heavy oak front door open downstairs, then shut again with a sonorous clunk, he remembered that he'd instructed Ricardo to take the four-by-four and go and collect Marianne. Ironic that he had been reflecting on his resistance to accepting help when he had just effectively hired a girl he had only recently met to come and live in his house and act as his housekeeper!

What had made her change her mind about accepting the post? he speculated. Perhaps it wasn't so difficult to deduce. Common sense had simply prevailed, and the plummeting temperatures had forced her to make a more sensible decision about her living and working arrangements after all. At least now he would not have her wellbeing on his conscience, as he imagined her standing at the roadside singing and ending up in hospital with hypothermia!

'Sounds like you've got company,' the therapist said cheerfully. 'Why don't you let me tidy up here, then I'll be on my way?'

* * *

'Ricardo… Take Miss Lockwood's coat and hang it up, if you would, and when you're done perhaps she would like a mug of hot chocolate to warm her up? We will be in the sitting room.'

Watching Ricardo help their visitor out of her too-large tweed overcoat and then leave, Eduardo skimmed his gaze over the medley of colourful clothing the girl wore underneath, and the curtain of long rippling hair over which she'd jammed the quite outrageously bright cerise woollen hat. He frowned.

'It might be a good idea to remove your hat too,' he suggested, the urge to smile suddenly too overwhelming to resist.

'Oh. I forgot.' Grabbing it off her head, Marianne stuffed it into the large bag made up of multi-coloured velvet squares that she'd temporarily left on the smooth marble floor in front of her.

For a few moments static electricity turned her light brown hair into a wild and silken tangle, and Eduardo could not help but stare at the arresting picture she made. A cinematic image of Mary Poppins the quintessential eccentric and pretty English nanny appeared in his mind. She sang too, he remembered, this time *without* amusement. Being bereft of the child he might have had, he was in no need of a nanny but a housekeeper. Someone who might help make his day-to-day living in self-imposed exile a little more bearable and smooth-running.

'Follow me,' he instructed, moving down a corridor

that led away from the generously proportioned hall, with its solid brass chandelier, and bypassing several closed doors before finally reaching one that was slightly ajar. Painfully and bitterly aware of his limp, he leaned a little too heavily on his walking cane and turned into the comfortably furnished sitting room. The only noise was the crackle and hiss of the blazing fire and the sedative ticking of the clock on the marble mantel. He stood aside to let Marianne precede him.

'Oh, how beautiful!'

Her gaze was not on the room itself, he saw, but on the incredible view that the tall curved windows with their parted drapes displayed. Eduardo sensed an arrow of pride shoot through him as he stared through the unadorned glass at the silhouette of majestic firs against the navy blue skyline. Stars were dotted about like splashed pinpricks of luminous paint, and a dazzling crescent moon hung suspended as though it were a bright magical toy controlled by a master puppeteer. He heard her softly appreciative gasp of pleasure.

'I told you that you would not be disappointed with the views, did I not? And it is nothing compared to what you will see in the daytime'

'I'm almost speechless at the sight of it!' Swinging her glance back in his direction, Marianne smiled at him with uncensored delight.

Again Eduardo had the disturbing sensation of his skin being too tight and hot to contain the avalanche of sensation that poured through him...a wave of sensual longing that was as powerful and unpredictable as El Niño...and prompted entirely by that bewitching smile. For a moment he could do nothing but stare. Automatically his mind took a snapshot of the captivating glowing features before him, and an old excitement that he had not experienced for ages pulsed strongly through his veins.

'We could be in another realm,' she enthused, green-gold eyes shining. 'However did you find such a place?'

'My mother grew up in this area. Whenever she brought me here as a child I loved it. So when I was looking for a house I knew immediately where I wanted it to be situated. I visited several before I was shown this place. As soon as I saw it I knew it was the right one.'

'You were right when you said it was remote.' As she secured the strap of her bag against her shoulder, Marianne's expression was thoughtful. 'When Ricardo was driving me here I didn't see another house or building for miles!'

'You are thinking maybe that it is *too* remote for your liking?'

'I don't think that at all. Seeing as I'm not someone who needs company all the time, being remote doesn't bother me. Besides...being around people too much can really get to you after a while, and I'd go crazy if I didn't have some peace and quiet to balance things out. Do you know what I mean?'

'Clearly I do—or else I would not be living here.' Eduardo smiled reluctantly, but he was genuinely surprised by the fact that she was apparently quite content with her own company. These days, when most people he observed seemed driven by the need for perpetual noise and distraction, it was positively *unusual.* 'Shall we continue our discussion sitting by the fire?'

Once they were ensconced in comfortable leather armchairs, Eduardo followed Marianne's mesmerised gaze to the dancing amber-gold flames. For a while companionable silence settled over them, like another softening blanket of snow on the desolate winter landscape outside.

'Warm enough?' he asked, almost reluctant to intrude upon the stillness and quiet with words.

Withdrawing her glance from the fire, she blinked at him as though momentarily forgetting who he was and why she was even there.

'Oh, yes…perfectly warm, thanks. I expect you're wondering why I changed my mind about taking you up on your offer,' she said in a rush, her pale, slender-fingered hands twisting together restlessly in the lap of her red wool dress. 'The truth is I suddenly realised that a change was what I needed after all. Being snowed in for three days certainly helped focus my mind on the subject! Although I was playing my music, doing what I loved, I was also in a bit of a rut. I figured it was time to try something different.'

'So you decided to ring me after all?' Linking his fingers steeple-like beneath his chin, Eduardo thoughtfully studied the pretty oval face and expressive hazel eyes before him. There were myriad conflicting emotions behind that arresting gaze that he couldn't help but wonder at. *Was she running away from something...some cruelty or unhappiness that she hadn't revealed? Something like an abusive relationship, perhaps?*

'I did. You—you didn't mind?'

'I would not have given you my card if I minded.'

'I just wanted to make sure.'

'And can I ask about the jobs you have had previously—before this?'

'Well. I...' Briefly Marianne's attention returned to the fire, where a hot coal sizzled brightly before settling more deeply into the nest of flames. 'I've worked in shops, mostly...a large clothing store, then a music store selling instruments and sheet music...that kind of thing.'

'You must have been in your element there.' Eduardo remarked, already knowing that music was a passion for her—the same as the career he had chosen had once been a passion for *him*. He quickly quashed the thought.

'I was.' The bewitching smile returned, naked and unguarded, and it was as though someone had brought a rare and beautiful orchid into the midst of a grey concrete prison cell. 'Look...I know I'm not exactly qualified to be a housekeeper, if you go by my previous employment, but I'm a fast learner, and I actually get great pleasure from doing the things that help make a house a home.'

'Talking of home...where was it you last lived,

Marianne?' he enquired, intrigued. 'A commune or a squat, perhaps?'

Her glance was perturbed. 'No. It was a house that I shared with somebody.'

'A boyfriend?'

'No…not a boyfriend. Can we talk about the job and what the daily routine is? I'd like to get a feel for things as soon as possible, so that I won't have to trouble you with too many questions.'

Reluctantly Eduardo curbed his curiosity. A businesslike approach to work was not what he had expected from someone who appeared as Bohemian as Marianne, but nonetheless it could hardly displease him, he mused silently. Not when he had begun to realise that established routines and a smooth-running household could sometimes help take the edge off the mental torture that plagued him, by acting as a sort of shield that could occasionally cushion him from the painful events of the past. For someone who had once been an inveterate risk-taker this was a revelation to him…even though he privately despised himself for succumbing to such appalling weakness.

'I have already briefed Ricardo about that. He is usually up and about early in the morning. Go and find him in the kitchen, and he will explain to you what to do. Help yourself to breakfast first. Ah…Ricardo. I was just telling Miss Lockwood that you will explain everything about her household duties in the morning.'

The tall, dark-eyed young man with a mop of curly

black hair, dressed in well-fitting denim jeans and a navy roll-necked sweater, smiled at Marianne, indicating his agreement to this plan.

'Now, drink up your hot chocolate,' Eduardo told her, envying his valet's easy, uncomplicated smile and wishing that he didn't privately feel like some invalid elder amongst them. Despite his injury he was actually still a strong and intelligent thirty-seven-year-old. 'Ricardo will bring in your baggage from the car and show you where your room is.'

'Thank you.' Rising to her feet at the same time as he did, Marianne gratefully nursed the mug of hot chocolate that Ricardo had placed in her hands.

She looked a little tired, Eduardo reflected. No doubt she would be anxious to get to her room, take stock, and mull over what the coming days and weeks living in this isolated place with her taciturn new employer would bring. When sufficient time had elapsed for her to realise what she had got herself into would she regret the decision she'd made? Coming to the conclusion that perhaps singing by the roadside was actually *easier*—no matter how inclement the weather?

Bitterly aware of his own shortcomings, and the way that depression and sometimes despair could descend like the blackest cloud, blotting out all sources of light within him and consigning him to being a blunt, unsparing, bad-tempered *bore*, Eduardo bit back a curse. Ricardo was used to his surly ways, but this fragile-looking girl was not.

Suddenly impatient with the downturn in spirits that his gloomy thoughts provoked, he turned away, intent on distracting himself with the book on an avant-garde Brazilian artist he was currently reading, leaving Marianne to the easygoing and no doubt more welcoming personality of his valet…

Marianne adored the room she'd been given. It was easily the warmest and most inviting bedroom she'd ever seen. After Ricardo had hefted her suitcase onto the neat double bed with its brass and iron bedstead, then carefully rested her beloved guitar in its case against the wall, she thanked him for his help and bade him goodnight. As soon as she was alone she examined her new surroundings with the kind of feminine delight she hadn't experienced in ages.

The plump white pillows and scalloped counterpane decorated with tiny embroidered pink roses on that inviting bed helped her finally succumb to the realisation of how tired she was—*mentally, physically and emotionally*… But fatigue was determinedly put aside as she concluded that this would indeed be the perfect room to return to after a hard day's work. As soon as she'd entered, its restful ambience had reached out to her and seeped into her thankful bones. And if there was ever a view to inspire contemplation and gratitude for life then Marianne was certain she would have to go far to beat the incredible vista that presented itself from the room's grand curved windows. The flowing red curtains parted, it was the same panoramic and haunting display that she'd seen downstairs in the sitting room.

Gazing out into the raw moonlit night, she felt an inexplicable sense of peace settle any lingering anxiety about what she'd done. All her bridges were in flames behind her, but it would be okay, she told herself. *Strangely enough, she had a good feeling about Eduardo De Souza.* He might be enigmatic, but he was kind too. She'd already seen many examples of his kindness in their short acquaintance, so she had nothing to fear.

Moving across the stripped oak floor that lovingly revealed the graceful patina of age, she opened a deep mahogany chest of drawers, with a slender glass vase displaying a slim bunch of tightly budded freesias on top of it, to find each drawer elegantly lined with scented floral silk. Inspecting the equally elegant double wardrobe, she found padded silk hangers and enough space inside to relegate her small and rather pathetic collection of multi-coloured clothing to looking like exhausted refugees.

To her great delight she then opened a door that she discovered led to the most enchantingly feminine bathroom. In pride of place gleamed a sparkling white claw-footed bath with gold taps, surrounded by shelves generously laden with pretty bottles of oil, bath crystals and expensive perfume. The smell that pervaded the room reminded her of standing in a beautiful garden in midsummer, when all the blooms were at the very peak of their beauty and scent. And in the dove-grey armoire by the side of a single stone-arched window there were neat rows of pristine white newly laundered towels and expensive linen.

Surveying both rooms, Marianne frowned in bewilderment. It was as though she were a welcomed invited *guest* in Eduardo's house instead of his new housekeeper! She was touched that he had gone to so much trouble to make her feel at home, but could hardly understand it. Then she cast her mind back to earlier on, when he'd asked her if she'd previously lived in a commune or a squat, and putting two and two together she realised that he probably *had* believed she'd been living quite rough. No doubt her busking in the street had confirmed that view. Clearly by giving her this lovely room to stay in he had wanted to show Marianne that he was sensitive to her situation. *But why should a man like him care about any adversity he'd assumed she'd endured?* Somehow it didn't tally with that hard, masculine, somewhat *remote* exterior. Again she thought what an enigma he was.

Sighing, Marianne drew her palm over her cheek—still warm from the fire downstairs—and moving her suitcase aside dropped down onto the bed. *She didn't want to deceive him…* Especially when he had freely offered her this chance to start over and make a new life for herself. At some point he deserved to know the truth. That she had married a man who had already been terminally ill when she'd met him, that he had been much older than her, that he and Marianne had become great friends through their shared passion for music and, on discovering that she had no family, he had married her to help give her the love and support that had long been lacking in her life.

And finally in his will he had bequeathed her his house, along with all his worldly goods. She hadn't been destitute, when Eduardo had imagined so. She'd actually not been badly off at all. *Until a couple of days ago, that was.* Now she really *did* need a job and a home. Because she had posted her house-keys to Michael and Victoria, instructed them to send any papers that needed signing care of the post office, and informed them that the house was now theirs. She was done with all the legal wrangling…it really wasn't worth the heartache.

Besides, from now on she aimed to be as *independent* as possible, and would not ever rely on anyone else for her welfare or her peace of mind again. Donal had provided a respite from that fierce struggle for a while, but now he was gone, and Marianne had concluded that a relationship was not something she would actively seek for a long, long time…if *ever. Not when it had been her experience that the people in her life either left, one way or another, or let her down.*

And in case her new employer might imagine she was some heartless little gold-digger who'd married an older man just for his money, she would let him know that Donal had genuinely loved her as she had loved him. All they had had together before his illness had finally killed him was six short months, but the man had cared more for her than her parents ever had… Tears washed into her already stinging eyes. It had been an emotional journey, packing up her things and leaving the only real home she'd ever really known behind, as well as a marriage that had ended so poignantly. But that phase of her life was over.

Rubbing at her moistened eyes, Marianne surged to her feet. The one thing she could do now was make sure Eduardo did not come to regret giving her this chance of a fresh start. Her impression was that the Brazilian—although kind—did not readily welcome strangers into his domain. Already she'd received the impression that he guarded his privacy—nearly all their conversations so far had been about Marianne's situation, not his own—and she wondered about that. Downstairs, as they had sat either side of the fire together, she had surreptitiously studied him as he talked. She had not been immune to the flare of pain in his fascinating blue eyes every now and then—had recognised the proud if not fierce need to hide it. Clearly the injury or illness that he had suffered was quite recent, and she definitely had the sense that the man could benefit from a little tender loving care.

It was fortunate for him that the one thing Marianne had learned about herself over the years was that it came very easily and naturally to her to help take care of others…

CHAPTER FOUR

DESPITE being in a completely strange environment, Marianne had had no trouble sleeping. Immediately on waking she roused herself and, barefoot, crossed the creaking polished floor to the windows. Although still dark, the sky was streaked with touches of hazy pink and grey, like soft pastel shades from an artist's paintbox. Morning light couldn't be far away, she guessed. The hard diamond glitter of the snow and frost shone so brightly in that dim half-light that the hills and woods were easily visible—the landscape just as breathtaking as it had been last night, she saw.

Crossing her arms over her chest, she shivered with something like anticipation at the prospect of the new day. Determined to be optimistic and hopeful, she told herself she was on the brink of a whole new phase in her life. It was *exciting*. Not something to dread. For a while she simply stood, contemplating the white sugar-frosted hills laid out before her like unblemished silvery patchwork, along with the tall, bare-branched trees whose tops disappeared into the sky, and fell into a sort of half dream.

What she saw could have been a magical scene from one of the illustrated pages of a child's book of fairy-tales. *She could even be the fairy princess, held captive in the tower and gazing out at her wicked captor's princely kingdom...*

'If you spent less time daydreaming, Marianne Lockwood, and more time focusing on your school-work, you might just turn out to be one less statistic in the unemployment figures!' A schoolteacher's exasperated tones came back to haunt her. Well, teachers didn't know *everything* she thought grimly.

Sometimes there were good reasons for a child's inattention—such as a very stressful home life, and a parent who was more or less drinking his life away. Daydreaming was essential for a child like that, Marianne could have told her teacher. *But she never did.* She'd borne the pain on her own.

Grimacing, reluctantly she turned away from the enticing view and headed into the bathroom. It was just after six, and her new boss had told her that Ricardo would be up and about early. When she found him, he would no doubt put her in the picture about what her new role as housekeeper entailed...

'Good morning. You are hungry?'

When she finally located the entrance to the huge country house kitchen, after exploring a ground floor seemingly full of endless corridors with unknown rooms and vestibules behind closed doors, it was to discover Ricardo frying bacon and eggs on the up-to-the minute shining replica of an old-fashioned range, wearing a blue and white striped apron over his jeans and sweat-shirt, and looking as if it was a task he was born to. Marianne's mouth dropped open in surprise. The room was filled with the most appetising smells of cooking, and her tummy rumbled appreciatively. Yesterday she'd barely eaten a thing, due to nerves and emotion, but now she was ravenous.

'Good morning—and, yes…I could *definitely* eat something!' Flicking her glance over the sturdy kitchen table laden with cereals, fruit, fresh bread, butter and a large jug of orange juice, she gave Ricardo a quizzical look. 'Do you normally go to all this trouble for breakfast in the morning, or is Mr De Souza joining us?'

'He is still sleeping and will eat later,' the valet explained, turning to survey her. 'You like bacon and eggs? I make traditional English especially for you.' He grinned. 'Please to help yourself to anything else you like.'

'Seeing as though it's not every day I get offered a cooked breakfast, how can I refuse?'

Pulling out a pine chair, Marianne sat at the table and poured a glass of orange juice. It was cold, tangy and refreshing. She could almost sense it doing her good. Good food had been low down on her agenda since Donal had died, and she hadn't really taken care of herself as well as she might. But now that she'd changed her situation things would be different, she vowed.

Recalling what Ricardo had said about his employer still sleeping, her slim brows drew together. 'Not that it's particularly late, but does Mr De Souza normally rise much later than you in the morning?' she asked.

Her companion went briefly still, but did not turn round. A second later she saw him flip the bacon in the pan with a steel spatula in an expert move that wouldn't shame a top chef.

'Sometimes yes, sometimes no,' he answered. 'You will see.' Scooping the eggs and bacon onto a heated plate that he retrieved from the oven with a striped padded mitt, he brought it over to the table and placed it in front of Marianne. 'Be careful…the plate is hot. Enjoy!'

'Thank you…I will.'

'I will make some coffee for us, then we can talk about your new job.'

'Okay.'

'You do not mind coffee? Perhaps you would prefer tea?'

About to fork some silky, perfectly cooked fried egg into her mouth, Marianne gave him a grateful shrug. 'Coffee is fine, thanks. By the way—this looks fantastic. Have you always been able to cook?'

'I learned at my mother's knee, as did all my brothers and sisters. Now, eat. I will make the coffee.'

From time to time, in between chewing mouthfuls of delicious food, Marianne watched the tall young man move round the kitchen as though it had always been his natural domain. Clearly domesticity neither fazed him nor emasculated him one iota. It was swiftly becoming apparent to her that he was perfectly comfortable in his own skin whatever he was doing, and already she intuited how fiercely loyal he was to his employer.

Continued private speculation made her wonder why Eduardo De Souza inspired such loyalty. Her curiosity surrounding the man increased. For instance, how come he didn't appear to have a wife? *Perhaps he did, and she had opted to stay in Brazil…or maybe he was divorced?*

Noticing that Marianne had finished eating, Ricardo whipped her plate away, leaving her with a cafetière of freshly brewed coffee, some sugar crystals in a tiny Willow pattern porcelain bowl, a matching jug of milk and a mug. He sat down opposite her, still—to her amusement—wearing his striped apron.

'Now we will talk,' he declared, pouring some delicious-smelling coffee into their waiting mugs.

'Has Mr De Souza had a housekeeper before?'

'Yes, in Rio de Janeiro where we are from, but not in this house. Here he hires outside people to come in and clean. It is very good that you are here, Marianne. I hope you will stay.'

At the doubt she detected in his accented voice, her curiosity was provoked even further. 'Why would I not stay?' she asked.

'I only meant that I hope you do not find the work too hard or the house too…too *alone* and wish to be somewhere else. That is all.'

'I see.' Focusing her hazel gaze on the handsome bronzed face before her, Marianne knew that was not what he'd meant at all, but decided to let it pass. 'And Mr De Souza…does he work from home?' she enquired.

'Yes. He is not working right now, but he does many—excuse me—*much* charity work.'

'Oh.' Was *that* why he had helped her, then? Because it was his mission in life to help those less fortunate? For a moment a sense of uncomfortable guilt washed over her. It wouldn't be wise to leave it too long before she explained her *true* circumstances, she thought. Or at least what had been her true circumstances before she'd recently changed them.

Recognising the wariness in Ricardo's gaze—no doubt in case her questions got a little *too* close to home—she curved her mouth in a genuinely warm smile to try and put him at ease.

'So…you'd better give me a rundown of what I'm supposed to do each day…then when we're finished talking I'll get cracking on that washing up.'

Her companion looked instantly relieved. 'That is a good plan. Well…first of all you must rise at four in the morning.'

'Four?' Seriously taken aback, Marianne stared.

'I am only kidding!' Dark eyes twinkling with merriment, Ricardo chuckled softly. 'The first thing you need to do in this unpleasantly cold weather is to light the fires. I make them all up before I go to bed.'

On the topmost floor of the eighteenth-century house later that morning, busy vacuuming acres of tastefully patterned hall carpet, Marianne briefly switched off the noisy machine to more closely examine a painting hanging on the flocked papered wall. The little gold plaque at the bottom of the frame told her that it was a portrait of the house at the turn of the century. Like today, the castellated roofs, turrets and surrounding landscape were cloaked in a sparkling blanket of pristine white snow. *Who had lived here then?* she speculated. Lord and Lady Somebody, no doubt. She pictured them for a moment, even added children to the imagined scene—a little boy and girl with cherubic faces, their lips sweetly bow-shaped and cheeks healthily pink.

Her mind lingered on the idea of having children of her own, but for a long time now she'd had a growing feeling that it was an experience that would never be hers. For who would love her and father her children now that Donal had gone? *Not that he—*

Abruptly she cut off the thought, weathered the silent emotional storm, and went back to her perusal of the painting. Had the owners hit on hard times, perhaps, and been forced to sell their beloved home to some filthy rich industrialist? It struck Marianne that her new employer must be exceedingly wealthy indeed to be able to purchase and live in such a grand dwelling. He was a philanthropist, Ricardo had intimated. Where had his wealth come from? Was it inherited?

In the midst of her reverie a door opened further along the now blissfully silent corridor. From it emerged the man whose image her thoughts seemed to be consumed by. His long legs were encased in smart black jeans, and he was wearing an expensive-looking navy cable-knit sweater. The dull gold of his hair—and it had to be said his noticeably pale complexion this morning—immediately drew Marianne's attention and concern.

'Good morning!'

'Next time start your vacuuming on the floor below, and do not come up to this floor until after I have risen and had my breakfast!'

Ignoring her friendly greeting, his voice rough with hostility, he swept by her, utilising his cane to walk, giving her a chilling ice-blue glare that she could immediately see was racked with pain. Her initial shock at his reply quickly ebbed, and concern over his appearance took precedence. Weeks of sitting by her husband's hospital bedside before he died had caused her to become intimately acquainted with such a look, and a spasm of fear gripped her and wouldn't let go.

Was he ill? Was it something serious? If so, why hadn't he or Ricardo told her the truth about what was wrong with him?

'Mr De Souza!' Hurrying after him, Marianne felt her heart hammer hard against her ribs at her intention to confront him.

'What is it?' Freezing in his tracks, he turned slowly to survey her. The pain in his glance had not lessened. Even the knuckles where he gripped the ivory handle of his cane were bleached white.

'I don't want to be intrusive…but is something the matter? I'd like to help if I can.'

'Help?' His mouth twisted scornfully. 'Are you in the business of performing miracles, then? Perhaps I should call you *Saint* Marianne?' His voice dripped disdain whilst the icy gaze that was as sharp as a steel blade all but dissected her. 'Why do you ask me this? Do you perhaps see another role for yourself here besides housekeeper?'

Words almost failing her, Marianne went rigid with embarrassment and shock. 'Of course not… I just—'

'Then my advice to you, *Miss* Lockwood, is to attend to your own business and let me attend to mine!'

Biting her lip, she turned away. But before she had the chance to go far, Eduardo addressed her again. And this time the lightly accented rich voice was rough with what sounded like genuine regret.

'I am sorry I spoke to you like that. But really…it is best if you do not speak to me when I first rise…at least not until I have had my coffee. I do not sleep well, and it takes a while for me to become human enough to converse with anyone. I am surprised Ricardo did not tell you that. But I fear he is always hoping for a miraculous change in me to come about. You ate breakfast, I trust?'

'Yes. Ricardo very kindly made me a cooked breakfast. I didn't eat much yesterday, what with one thing and another, and it was—it was most welcome.'

Inside her chest, Marianne's racing heartbeat had barely calmed at all, and to be honest she couldn't help but be wary of another explosion of irritability. Irritability she was all but certain was fuelled by pain and, as Eduardo had indicated, lack of sleep. She made a mental note not to vacuum until much later in the day in future.

'Good. I will let you get on with your work, then.'

'I'm—I'm sorry that you do not sleep well. I'll remember your instructions not to clean here until you're up and about.'

'That would be appreciated.'

His compelling blue eyes briefly skimmed over her face before he continued on his way down the corridor, his limp definitely more pronounced this morning, renewing Marianne's concern. But—wiser now—she didn't allow her gaze to linger, and quickly returned to her housework in case he thought she might be watching him…

'Here.' A glass of water and two white capsules were placed in front of Eduardo at the breakfast table, next to his coffee cup. Behind him, Ricardo hovered close, his familiar face concerned. 'You do not look good. I can tell you had a rough night. I know you do not like to rely on them, but maybe you should consider taking your painkillers this morning? They might give you some relief.'

'I'm not feeble, for God's sake—and you know what you can do with those!'

Shoving the pills back into the younger man's hand, Eduardo wished he could control the cantankerous mood that was upon him, but he could not. He had barely had even an hour's sleep during the night, and his eyes felt as if they were burning holes in their sockets. Coupled with the relentless knifing agony in his leg, he could hardly be expected to be at his best, could he? As the day went on he knew the pain would ease a little...*if* he could relax sufficiently enough. Then the discomfort would ebb *without* the need for painkillers. But right now that was like hoping for the impossible.

Into his consciousness stole another thought. For some inexplicable reason he recalled the newest addition to his household softly enquiring if he was all right and if she could help, and a longing so compelling and powerful surged through him that he was almost overcome...*almost*. Quickly he caught himself, regained the tight rein he usually kept on his emotions. What the hell was he thinking of? She might smell sweeter than a spring garden after a summer shower, but the fact was she couldn't possibly help him—and he would hate her to be labouring under the delusion that she could.

He had only *one* use for an attractive female right now, and as far as that was concerned he would be utterly *crazy* to think of his little roadside waif in that way! His honour simply wouldn't allow it. Not when he had offered her a job and a home, and probably the first safe place she had known for some while.

Getting to his feet, he reached for his walking cane,

his glance swinging briefly to Ricardo. 'I didn't mean to chew your head off.' He grimaced. 'You know how it is.'

'One day it will change for the better, I am certain.'

The compassion and understanding that shone from the other man's eyes, undimmed and loyal as ever, almost made Eduardo stumble. Leaving his home and family behind in Rio de Janeiro, Ricardo had unquestioningly chosen to accompany his employer to a new unknown life in England, with no certainty of when he would be returning home. He had merely been absolutely convinced that after the tragedy that had taken Eduardo's wife and unborn child he would need a familiar face to turn to whenever things got rough. Ricardo would be that face. He had served the De Souza family since he had come to them from the poor slums of the city at seventeen. They had given him a job and a home, and he saw it as his proud duty to continue to serve until his boss told him different.

Now, at the memory of all that had transpired, the burning inside Eduardo's throat made him swallow hard.

'I cannot agree that things will change for the better, my friend. How could that be possible? The fact is I am damned...*damned* for eternity...and whether my physical pain heals or not nothing will alter that.'

Not commenting immediately, Ricardo turned towards the kitchen worktop, picked up a nearby cloth and rubbed it over the already gleaming marble that Marianne had cleaned earlier. 'I do not think Eliana... your wife...would want you to suffer like this...to *blame* yourself for so long,' he murmured. 'I do not think she would want that at all.'

'Let's drop the subject, shall we? I'm going to my office now. I've got plenty of work to do, and no doubt that will help distract my mind from dwelling on less than pleasant things.'

'If you are going to your office then I will bring you the newspapers and another cup of coffee.'

'Thanks.' His voice gruff, Eduardo started to move towards the door. Before he reached it he paused for a moment. 'By the way…how did my new housekeeper do this morning?' he asked.

Ricardo's expression immediately lightened. 'I can tell already that she is a hard worker,' he answered. 'She is skinny, but I think tough too.'

'Well…let me know if there are any problems,' Eduardo threw over his shoulder as he left. And, in spite of his irritability and pain, he was unable to stop his lips from twitching at his valet's rather blunt, yet in his view *well-meant* description of Marianne as 'skinny but 'tough'.

There was a tentative knock at his office door. Tearing his glance from the neat rows of text on the computer screen in front of him—an e-mail from an international children's charity, thanking him for his continued support and generosity—Eduardo rotated his shoulders to ease the spasm of tension that flashed between his shoulderblades.

'Come in!' he called out.

'Sorry to disturb…'

It was Marianne, her cheeks flushed from being near some kind of heat, her light brown hair caught up in a precarious topknot that, judging by the silken tendrils floating free down the sides of her face, appeared in imminent danger of collapsing at any moment. Wearing a navy and white striped apron over scarlet cotton trousers and a man's baggy cream sweater that all but drowned her small slim frame, she looked delicate and somehow inexplicably appealing all at the same time. *Had she been wearing that outfit this morning, when he'd met her in the corridor?* Eduardo could not swear to it. He had been too taken aback by her offer of help, and the gentleness and concern in her almond-shaped hazel eyes to notice.

'What is it?' he asked interestedly, the tension and fatigue he had been battling with somehow forgotten.

'I'm sorry it's a bit late, but lunch is ready. I've been baking bread and making soup, and it took longer than I thought.'

'You have been baking bread *and* making soup? What kind of soup?'

'Leek and potato… It's really good for you, especially in this weather. I'm sure you'll like it. Anyway…' Her expression was suddenly shy, as if she'd assumed too much and was embarrassed by her own enthusiasm. 'Where would you like to eat? Up here in your office? Or I could lay a place in the dining room if that's what you'd prefer.'

'Where are *you* going to eat? In the kitchen?'

'Yes. Ricardo's gone to town for some supplies, and he said he'll have his food later.'

Suddenly tired of his own morose company, and the thought of home-made bread and soup enticing him more than he would ever have believed possible, Eduardo reached for his cane and stood up. 'I will join you in the kitchen,' he answered firmly.

'All right, then.' The rather sombrely furnished room with its dark cherry leather sofas and crammed bookshelves was suddenly lit by her golden smile and—still smiling—Marianne stood back to let Eduardo precede her out of the room…

CHAPTER FIVE

MARIANNE had been thinking about miracles. She knew they existed because she had prayed hard for someone kind to come into her life and then Donal had appeared. Now, as she surveyed the lean-angled, handsome face on the opposite side of the table from her, with its preoccupied and enigmatic air, she silently pondered on why such a man needed a miracle in his life. Again she considered the disturbing possibility that he had a life-threatening illness, and in the middle of lifting her spoon to her lips she felt her throat lock tight and her appetite flee.

'This is very good.' Having no such similar dilemma, Eduardo glanced up appreciatively from sampling his own soup. His piercing blue eyes bored into hers, and Marianne's stomach fluttered hard.

'Thank you.'

Tearing off a hunk of bread from the generous-sized, still warm loaf on the bread board, he experimentally chewed some, then laid the rest on his side plate.

'You really know how to cook. This is delicious too.'

'They say necessity is a great teacher. There wasn't much money around when I was growing up, but my parents had a small vegetable patch for a while, and one year we had an abundance of leeks, carrots and turnips. Something had to be done with them. Soup was the easiest solution. After that I got quite interested in cooking and experimented a little. Making bread was therapeutic, too, I found.'

The interest in her companion's face deepened. 'I thought you had no parents?'

'That was a long time ago.' Feeling her chest tighten, Marianne scooped a small portion of soup into her mouth, then fell silent.

'What happened to them?'

Clearly not deflected from pursuing the subject, Eduardo stilled as he waited to hear her answer.

'My mother left when I was fourteen to go to America with a man she'd been having an affair with. My father—?'

'Yes?'

'Right now my father is probably lying dead or drunk beneath a bridge somewhere in London. Tower Bridge was a particular favourite. At least…that was where I saw him last.'

'When was that?'

Marianne lowered her gaze. 'About three years ago. He was—*is*—a hopeless alcoholic. That's why my mother couldn't stay with him. Eat your soup. It will get cold.'

Pushing to her feet, she strode across the ample-sized

kitchen to the butler sink to pour herself a glass of cold water. Her throat felt as if it had swelled to twice its size at the tormenting tide of childhood memory that washed over her. Talking about it only deepened her distress.

As if realising the discrepancy in her parenting of her only daughter, her mother had beseeched Marianne to go with her to America. But even at the tender age of fourteen years old she'd found she could not abandon the dejected wreck bent on self-destruction that her father had become. Not when at the back of her mind somewhere had been more *loving* memories of him hugging her, playing childish games with her when she was little, calling her his angel. Afterwards, when there had just been the two of them in a house that was no longer a home, there were sadder, heartrending recollections—him crying unbearably, begging Marianne to forgive him for losing his business, needing to drink to dull the pain of driving her mother away.

Yes, she understood *why* her mother hadn't been able to stay with such a man—even at fourteen she'd seen that she was in an untenable situation—but that hadn't made it any easier for her to cope. And it hadn't lessened the sense of betrayal she felt either. The brutal reality of being left behind to be responsible for a man who no longer seemed to care whether he lived or died as long as he could have the next drink was something that she would *never* forget.

'Marianne?'

'I'm sorry. I just needed some water.' Returning to the

table, she sat down. Inadvertently catching Eduardo's eye, she made a valiant attempt to smile.

'You should eat something,' he said brusquely, but the expression in his disturbing glance was compassionate and steady, and even more unsettling was the supreme difficulty Marianne had in tearing her gaze from his. 'Children need fathers…I am sorry that yours was not able to care for you as he should have done.'

'Do you have parents? Siblings?' she asked.

'My parents live in Leblon, which is west of Ipanema where I have my beach house. They are retired now. Unfortunately I was not blessed with brothers or sisters. I am their only son.'

'I longed for a brother or sister when I was young,' Marianne confessed, 'but perhaps it was best that there was only me in the long run. Parenting didn't come naturally to my mum and dad, I'm afraid.'

After this silence reigned, and she was grateful that Eduardo did not quiz her further on her unhappy past. She guessed that he appreciated her own perceived lack of curiosity where he was concerned. Her assessment that he was the most private of men was becoming more evident. Understanding that, she would not bombard him with intrusive questions. He just given her a job and a home, and she would respect his need to withhold certain information. *Even if the fact he might be ill secretly ate away at her and caused her imagination to run riot.* Maybe she could discreetly ask Ricardo about it if she got the chance?

'I generally take a walk in the grounds after lunch.' Reaching for his walking cane, Eduardo rose from the table. 'Would you care to join me?'

Patting her lips with her linen napkin, Marianne glanced longingly out at the snowy scene evident through the window. Above them was a cloudless cobalt sky, the kind of winter sunshine that skiers were used to in the Alps, and sparkling frost and snow carpeted everything. In truth, she would have liked nothing better than to walk in such an inviting magical landscape. But she was conscious that she was now an employee of this man…*not* his guest.

'I would love a walk…but I was planning on dusting and polishing in some of the rooms—there's so many of them it will probably take most of the afternoon to get round.'

'Dusting and polishing can wait. It's not important,' her companion countered a touch irritably, already making his way to the door. 'I will meet you at the back entrance in fifteen minutes. You have the necessary footwear to walk in? If not, there is an array of boots in the mud room. I am sure you will find a pair your size.'

'Thanks…but I have boots of my own that I brought with me.'

'Good.' His glance briefly flicked over her. 'Fifteen minutes!' he called over his shoulder, and he looked away, his broad back in the navy cable-knit sweater the last glimpse Marianne had of his imposing physique as he left.

* * *

It had started to snow again. *How many more days would the sky continue to empty its frozen cargo down upon the earth?* One minute Eduardo welcomed the deadening silence it left in its wake in a landscape in which he'd deliberately sought escape from the rest of the world and the next…the next he wrestled with an irrepressible longing for the warmth, sounds, smells and the sheer sense of *aliveness* that denoted his birthplace.

Releasing a sigh, he glanced sideways at his walking companion to see that Marianne's bright woolly hat was covered in rapidly melting crystals of ice. There were two spots of intense pink staining the pale satin of her cheekbones too, and her breath made little plumes of steam as she breathed.

'If you are too cold we will go back inside,' he offered, strangely reluctant to do any such thing.

'I'm quite happy.' she answered, hazel eyes shining. 'The thing about getting cold is that you can always get warm again. What's up there?'

They had crossed a wooden latticework bridge over the moat, its previously peeling and weathered green paintwork having recently been restored by Ricardo, and now they faced a fork in the road. One path led deeper into the extensive grounds of the house, and the other wound its snowy way into the thickness of the surrounding forest. It was this path that Marianne's gloved hand pointed towards.

Eduardo shrugged. 'The forest...I have never personally followed the trail to see where it goes.'

'Are you serious? Whenever I'm somewhere I haven't been before and I see a bend in the road—especially in the countryside—I wonder what adventures may be waiting round the corner! Aren't you at all curious?' As she came to an abrupt stop, the incredulity on her face was plain to see.

'Not so far,' he admitted. 'And as for adventures... they are not something I personally crave.' Almost without his realising it, Eduardo's glance travelled down towards his injured leg and the cane he leaned on to help support it.

'You mean because of your leg?' Marianne deduced.

So far she had been extraordinarily polite when it came to not enquiring about his injury, but now he himself had inadvertently brought the subject to her attention. Momentarily his exasperation with himself knew no bounds. A large black crow streaked across the sky, cawing. The discordant sound seemed to amplify the tension inside him. Worryingly, the tight control that he kept coiled inside threatened to unravel at the claustrophobic and discomfiting sensation of being under siege.

'The weather seems to be worsening. Perhaps it would be best if we returned to the house.' His voice sounded cold and disconnected even to his own ears.

'Does it give you a lot of pain?' Gentle concern shone from Marianne's eyes, and Eduardo felt frighteningly cornered. Snow continued to fall—fat icy flakes bombarding them, turning them into human snowmen. 'I would rather not discuss it, if you don't mind.'

'I only ask because I'm concerned.'

'Then please do not be!'

'I'm sorry if you think I'm invading your privacy. I don't mean to. It's just that—well…if you're ill, and it's something serious, it might be helpful for me to know that.'

'That is where you are *wrong*!' Now Eduardo was furious—at her, and at himself for suggesting she accompany him in the first place. 'I have heard that the offspring of alcoholics often feel the need to try and fix the problems of others. Please do not make the arrogant mistake of thinking that you can fix mine!'

And with that he found himself turning back towards the bridge they had just crossed, more self-conscious than ever that his injured leg impeded more rapid progress, and angry too because he had lost control and lashed out at Marianne personally. Her father was lying either dead or drunk under a bridge somewhere, and she'd clearly been traumatised by an upbringing with parents that he deduced had been too self-absorbed even to notice their daughter's distress…else why had she ended up singing at the roadside for a living? He simply had no right to vent at her as he just had, whether he was feeling overwhelmed or *not*.

He didn't think that he had ever disliked himself more

than he did right then. Except for the day of the accident, that was…that day he had positively *hated* himself…

Marianne was certain she must have polished the same spot on the grand mahogany sideboard at least a dozen times, if not more. As the light was leeched from the sky and fires lit and curtains drawn Eduardo's angry words bounced round her brain like a ping-pong ball run amok. *I've heard that the offspring of alcoholics often feel the need to fix the problems of others…* As well as putting her firmly in her place, the brutal words had sent her thoughts hurtling towards the past again…but this time with startling new insight. *Was that what she had tried to do with everyone she loved?* Fix their problems? As if she didn't *deserve* happiness unless she could somehow make everything right for everyone else?

Was that why she had stayed with her father instead of seizing a chance of happiness with her mother in a new country, with a different life from the painful existence she'd endured for so long? Her mother still wrote to her, pleading with her to join her and Geoff—her new husband—in California…*especially* now that Donal was gone. In her last reply, nine months ago, Marianne had told her that she definitely wanted to remain in England, and at the back of her mind she had found herself thinking *just in case dad needs me*. But she hadn't seen her father for three years, and had lost all contact.

It wasn't easy to keep tabs on where he was when he had effectively become a vagrant, and in the end the constant worry and fruitless searching had all but made her ill. But maybe there was some kind of organisation or agency she could contact to help her locate him? And if not what about the hospitals, just in case he had—? Her mind wouldn't let her go there. Chewing anxiously down on her thumb, she tasted the bitter tang of beeswax polish and withdrew it almost instantly.

'Marianne?'

'Ricardo… Sorry—I didn't hear you come in.'

Stepping into the beautiful library, with its polished wooden floor, various exotic rugs and tightly packed dark wood bookshelves crammed with a myriad books that he had told Marianne during their tour of the house had been shipped over from Brazil, the young man thoughtfully crossed his arms.

'Mr De Souza would like some coffee. I could have made it for him, but he told me he would like you to see to it.'

'Of course.' Gathering up the soft dustcloth and polish she'd been using, Marianne moved towards the door—but halfway across the room she stopped, frowned, and shrugged her shoulders.

'I think he's angry with me, Ricardo.'

'Why should that be so?'

'I asked him about his leg…if it was hurt because he was ill or something. He didn't like it and he got quite cross with me. I'm quite anxious that he doesn't think I'm some kind of interfering busybody.'

A little crease appeared in the coffee-coloured skin between Ricardo's dark brows. 'You have to understand something about Eduardo De Souza. He is a man who—' He glanced briefly upwards, as if searching for the right words and how to say them in a language that was not his native one. 'A man who does not welcome people looking into his private life. If he chooses not to explain something…then he has his reasons. I ask that you respect those reasons even if you do not know what they are.'

'And I *do* respect them! I see that he doesn't want his privacy invaded, and God knows I understand that, but I ask you—what's wrong with expressing concern if you see that someone is in pain or…or difficulty?'

'You have a kind heart, and that is certainly not a crime, Marianne. You will just have to take things one day at a time and eventually…gradually…Eduardo will see that you are a genuine person and do not want to make trouble for him.'

Now Ricardo was smiling, and although Marianne was initially reassured, her stomach still clenched uncomfortably at the thought of facing her employer again and possibly seeing suspicion and mistrust in his eyes.

'I hope I haven't kept you waiting too long. I've brought you some biscuits too.'

In the sitting room, with the fire cosily crackling, she laid the round patterned tray in front of Eduardo on the coffee table, waiting until he'd folded the broadsheet newspaper he'd been reading and laid it next to him on the sofa. He tunnelled his fingers through his hair, then rubbed a hand round his jaw. It was studded with five o'clock shadow and made him look slightly disreputable, Marianne noticed. The sleeves of his cable-knit sweater were rolled halfway up his muscled forearms, and she saw the fine dark blond hairs that dusted his skin.

'You haven't kept me waiting,' he said gruffly, helping himself to coffee and a digestive biscuit at the same time. 'How are you getting on?' he added, before taking a sip of the aromatic brew in his cup.

'Getting on?' Unprepared, Marianne's nervous glance collided into his, and her stomach jolted so violently at the sight of those searching blue eyes with their straight dark lashes that she could barely think straight for a moment.

'The work is not too hard for you?' Eduardo elucidated.

'Not at all. I'm enjoying it, in fact. This house is a joy! Every room I go into is a revelation.'

'An *adventure*?' His serious, well-shaped lips formed the wryest of smiles and Marianne sensed hot embarrassed colour rush into her face.

'I suppose you think that's childish?'

'You think someone like me is incapable of understanding the appeal of adventure? When I was your age I would have equalled your desire for the unexpected... the turn in the road that might yield the happy unknown. Unfortunately, sometimes life yields the not so pleasant unexpected adventure too, and it can dampen one's youthful hopefulness…even destroy it for ever. Why don't you sit down for a moment and take a break?'

Pondering his surprisingly revealing comments, Marianne felt her body tense uncomfortably. 'I'm sorry if some bad things happened to taint your optimism. I know what that feels like. But ultimately—despite the things that go wrong and hurt us—we have to go on and try to make the best of our lives, don't you think?'

'What if you are to blame for causing hurt to someone else?' Eduardo immediately came back at her, looking as if he genuinely wanted her answer.

'Then there is always forgiveness… Not just from the person you hurt but more importantly to *yourself*.'

'Have you forgiven your father for being a drunk and not taking proper care of you?'

Hearing the bitter edge to his words, Marianne frowned, wondering if he had hurt someone who *hadn't* forgiven him, and was still living with too much guilt and regret over whatever had happened. 'In my heart I honestly try to,' she replied carefully. 'I pity him, if you want to know. Alcoholism is a disease, and when it gets a hold it's very hard to recover from it. He turned to drink in the first place because of the pressure on him to be a success—something our culture perpetually promotes. When we can't live up to it we call ourselves failures. We don't need outside forces to punish us when we can do it quite beautifully on our own…my dad being a case in point.'

'Are you going to sit down for a while?'

Still pondering their revealing exchange, and perhaps a little wary that she had said too much, she quickly declined. 'I won't, if you don't mind. I need to go and prepare dinner. Ricardo has a pair of wild ducks a local farmer gave him. I thought I'd make a nice orange sauce to go with them, and serve it with French beans and mashed potato.'

'A culinary delight to be anticipated with much pleasure, I am sure.'

'Are you suggesting that it's not refined enough for your taste?'

'I was not being droll, Marianne. You forget I have already sampled your cooking and know that you are quite expert. I only meant what I said as a compliment.'

'Oh.' She had been unconsciously twirling a long strand of her hair round and round her finger, feeling increasingly on edge at not knowing what to expect from this man from one moment to the next. At the reassurance in his words she released the soft tendril she'd been toying with and attempted a smile. To the side of her, in its impressive marble surround, the fire hissed invitingly, and if Eduardo's company had been *less* likely to put her on her guard Marianne would gladly have accepted his invitation to sit down and take a break. But, perversely, she was also looking forward to cooking her first real dinner in this lovely old house, and putting her worries and concerns aside for a while.

'Well, I'd better carry on, then. Dinner will be ready around seven. Is that all right with you?'

'That is fine. We need to talk about your remuneration. We have not discussed it yet. Perhaps after dinner you would see me in my study?'

'Okay.'

It was as if the door of informality Eduardo had opened earlier when he had cordially invited her to join him had been shut firmly in her face. In its place formality suddenly reigned, and as she walked back down the long echoing corridor towards the grand staircase that led downstairs Marianne silently admitted that she didn't like it. She didn't like it one bit…

CHAPTER SIX

EDUARDO had wanted to mention the fact that he regretted his earlier outburst when they had been walking together in the grounds. But then he'd considered that if he set a precedent he could well be apologising to Marianne the entire time she worked for him. Better that she quickly learned how to adapt to his mood swings and cope with them as best she could. But perversely it also *irked* him that she hadn't accepted his invitation to sit a while and talk.

With the excellent dinner she had cooked behind them, Eduardo now faced her across the polished expanse of the impressively large desk in his study. *Was he deliberately putting up barriers between them?* It would not surprise him. Not when he sensed himself becoming more and more captivated by her and apprehensive of where that might leave him.

'This is the figure I had in mind,' he said out loud, pushing the piece of paper he had scribbled on towards her.

Peering at what he had written, Marianne leaned back silently in her chair.

'Well?' Impatiently Eduardo tapped his pen on the blotter.

'It's too much.'

'We are not going down *that* route again, are we?'

'I'm not being deliberately difficult, Mr De Souza—'

'Eduardo.'

She flushed a little. 'Is it right that I call you Eduardo when I'm an employee of yours…not a friend? It wouldn't seem right. Anyway…what I meant was what you're offering seems far too generous. Especially when you consider that I'm living in, and all my meals are included as well.'

Looping some soft strands of dark honey hair round her small ear, Marianne lifted her chin. All of a sudden Eduardo's entire attention was commanded by her mouth…her pretty, sweetly shaped lips in which he'd just detected an intriguing tremble. Erotic heat poured violently through his bloodstream, and never had he known such instantaneous torrid desire grip him with quite such commanding force before. It took him a moment to collect himself enough to speak.

'There are not many employees, I am sure, who would protest about being paid too generously,' he commented dryly. 'You are certainly one of a kind, Marianne.'

'That may be so. But, like I told you before, I'm not a charity case. You should pay me the rate you would normally pay someone taking up this position.'

'How do you know that this is *not* the rate I would normally pay?'

'I don't. But I think it's in your nature to be kind…to help those you see as less fortunate. All I ask is that you pay me the true rate the post commands. That will be more than good enough.'

She believed it was in his nature to be kind. The idea almost froze Eduardo in his seat. After all that had happened, kind was the *last* word he would have used to describe his nature. Peevishly, and to prove her wrong, he snatched the paper towards him and wrote down a different figure—deducting at least five per cent from the usual housekeeper salary Marianne had suggested he pay her. He pushed it back to her and got up from his seat.

Examining what he had written, he heard her softly murmur, 'Thank you.'

Watching her stand, he let his gaze hungrily scan her slender upright figure, noticing that the neck of the too large cream sweater had slid tantalisingly down over a pale smooth shoulder…a perfectly *edible* and bewitchingly feminine shoulder. Eduardo stared, his heart thudding. Not only did he feel aroused, but his body *and* mind were suddenly consumed with one passionate, compelling idea—a need and a desire he seemed to have no control over. And he was quite aware that made him vulnerable in an area where he had actively sought to protect himself—*feelings and emotions.*

Marianne started to walk towards the door. 'Ricardo

is going out to the woodshed to get some kindling for the morning. I need a breath of air, and I said I'd go and help him. Excuse me.'

'Marianne?'

'Yes?' She stopped and turned.

'You are getting on well with Ricardo, I take it?'

'Yes, I am.'

'You like him?'

'What's not to like? He's a very pleasant young man, and easy to get along with.'

'You talk as though you were twenty years older than him, instead of there being just a year's difference in age between you!'

She frowned and folded her arms, looking uncomfortable. 'I expect I come across as older in the way I speak sometimes, because I'm used to taking charge of things. Habit, I suppose…'

'Did he inform you that he is going to be away for a few days from tomorrow? He is due some time off, and is meeting up with friends in London who have travelled over from Brazil.'

'He did mention it…yes.'

'And you are not uneasy at the idea of being alone with me in the house while he is gone?'

Her eyes fixed candidly and unwaveringly on Eduardo's face. 'Why should I be? You're my employer as well as—as well as a friend…I feel perfectly safe with you'

'I am gratified that you admit to owning me as a

friend at last, when earlier you seemed to discount that and refer to me only as your employer!'

'We were starting to become friends before you offered to help me out with a job and a home…weren't we?' She visibly flushed as she said this.

'Well…' His desire seeming inconveniently and almost *painfully* to increase, Eduardo affected a dismissive shrug. 'You had better go and find Ricardo, then, and get on with what you were doing.'

'Do you need anything before I go?' Marianne asked innocently.

Eduardo almost prayed out loud to the Mother of Guadeloupe for strength at the vivid pictures that came into his mind following such a question, and his voice was gruffer than he meant it to be when he answered. 'No. I do not need anything at all. If I do…Ricardo can attend to it when he returns.'

'Okay.'

Stepping outside into the corridor, Marianne closed the door quietly behind her…

Having prided herself on surviving without too much mishap, providing meals and beverages throughout the day for Eduardo and herself after Ricardo had left for London, as well as attending to the rest of the housework, Marianne fixed her sights on a long hot bath and then relaxing with a good book. *But she wasn't entirely at her ease.*

Two things had unsettled her. Firstly, the realisation

that for someone who seemed so interested in a photographic exhibition that he would visit it more than once Eduardo didn't seem to have any personal photographs of his own. There were certainly none on display in the house, and that struck her as rather odd. Maybe for some reason Eduardo was trying to *lose* his past? she speculated. Or at least leave it behind? Secondly, earlier on that afternoon he had had a visit from his physiotherapist. The man had seemed pleasant enough, but after he had gone Marianne had knocked on the sitting room door to offer Eduardo a cup of tea, and the strain on his face and the faint beads of sweat standing out on his forehead had shocked her. She hadn't had to ask if he was in pain. The evidence had been staring her right in the face.

As she had been about to leave him to go and make the tea, she hadn't been able to help turning back and saying crossly, 'I thought a therapist was meant to *ease* pain…not cause it!'

'What do you suggest I do?' Eduardo mocked bitterly, lifting his injured leg onto the couch and barely suppressing a groan. 'Fire him?'

'I'm sorry,' she murmured, hurrying forward to help him, then felt redundant when she saw that he had already settled himself quite satisfactorily, without any aid from her. 'I don't mean to interfere.'

'You have appointed yourself my personal guardian angel I see,' he commented, and before Marianne knew what was happening he had captured her hand, held it, then stroked her knuckles with the slightly roughened pad of his thumb.

The sensual heat that ricocheted through her was like a ruthless thief, stealing every scrap of moisture from her mouth and making her heart hammer. Inside her cotton bra, her nipples stiffened hotly and painfully. Never before had she experienced such a torrid reaction to a man's touch. Her bones had turned fluid as a river, and it was hard to see how she remained standing she was so shaken.

Before she could come to her senses Eduardo released her hand to fix a cushion more securely behind his back. Then he smiled at her...*really* smiled...and it was like being miraculously treated to a stunning glimpse of the *real* man behind the aloof, pain-filled mask that he normally wore. Her reason bound and gagged for debilitating seconds, Marianne experienced an almost uncontrollable urge to touch the skin round his jaw. She instinctively knew it would be like rough velvet. She wanted to smooth back the tantalising lock of dark wheat hair that had strayed boyishly onto his brow. So stunned was she by the power of that desire, she had to bite her lip and clench her hands to stop her from following its forceful command.

'I think that cup of tea would be most welcome now,' Eduardo remarked, with just a hint of an amused curl of his lip, as though he was quite aware of the effect he had had on her and—shockingly—did not regret it in the least.

Once she had reached on the other side of the closed

sitting room door, Marianne had gratefully breathed again with more ease, leaning back against the oak panelling to compose herself. But it had been quite a few moments before she had been able to move freely again. Eduardo's electrifying touch had all but set her on fire, and had been an utter revelation. Closing her eyes, she'd put her hand up to her throat and dreamily relived it again. At last, willing herself to move, she had dazedly made her way back downstairs to the kitchen.

In the early hours of the morning, with the long shadows from the stately trees reflected into the room by the moonlight and the ticking of the bedside clock for company, Marianne was wide awake, and about as far from sleep as it was possible to be. With a resigned sigh she switched on the pretty fringed lamp on the cabinet next to her. Punching her feather pillow a couple of times to reinstate its plumpness, she arranged it more comfortably behind her back, then reached for her book. But her gaze couldn't help straying towards her guitar, still in the same position against the wall where Ricardo had left it for her.

It seemed like eons since she had played. Who would she disturb if she strummed a few gentle chords? Ricardo was away, and Eduardo's rooms were on the floor above Marianne's. Swinging her legs out of bed, her book discarded, quiet excitement gripped her at the idea of making music again. Perhaps if the snow started to disperse she could visit the folk club and get to do some singing?

Just as she was reaching towards the instrument a loud thud—much too loud to ignore in the haunting quiet of the house—sounded clearly from the floor above.

Turning rigid with fright, Marianne could swear she heard her own heartbeat echo round the room. Then, with all thoughts of three a.m. ghosts or departed spirits determinedly quashed, another far more frightening thought galvanised her into action. Hurrying back to the bed, she grabbed up her dressing gown, quickly pulled it on over her nightdress, then slid her feet into her slippers. Stepping outside into the dimly lit corridor outside her room, shivering now not at any *sound* but at the almost uncanny silence that enveloped her, she didn't linger. Moving like a will-o'-the-wisp to reach the imposing staircase, and with her heart in her mouth, she urgently ascended the carpeted steps to the upper floor.

Hesitating for the scantest second, Marianne rapped loudly on the door to Eduardo's rooms.

'You may as well come in!' he answered, his voice definitely disgruntled.

Bracing herself, she entered. The fire that must have been blazing brightly in the marble fireplace earlier on that evening had died to flickering orange embers, but even though all the lamps were turned off the heavy drapes had been left undrawn. Illuminating moonlight helped Marianne locate Eduardo almost instantly. Sitting upright on a sofa, he was nursing what looked like a cut hand. Immediately she saw the cause. A broken lamp lay drunkenly on the heavy oak coffee table in front of him, and shards of glass from the bulb were everywhere. The moonlight made them glitter like tinsel.

'You've hurt your hand! Let me see.'

Not bothering with a greeting, Marianne flew across the room to his side, gently taking his bloodied hand in her own. Withdrawing a clean folded handkerchief from her dressing gown pocket, she examined the perfectly neat long cut that was oozing blood for any evidence of glass, then carefully wrapped his hand in the white linen square. Hearing his ragged breath, easily sensing the tension in his body, she felt her stomach grip tight with concern. She glanced up enquiringly into his eyes. Eduardo stared back at her with a burning gaze hot enough to melt steel. It seared her soul with its almost *uncanny* power, the reddened rims round his eyes and raw pain that she witnessed there almost making her gasp. *He resembled a man who had not either slept nor seen daylight for weeks and had all but reached the end of his endurance.* Fear and concern flooded her insides.

'I am sorry if I woke you,' Eduardo murmured, scraping his hand with frustration though dark wheat hair that had already received plenty of similar rough treatment, she saw. 'I did not realise that you would have heard my stupid accident with the lamp. I got up too suddenly and my leg did not support me for a moment. I fell towards the table—my aim to sweep the lamp out of the way as I went down. Instead I landed on it, and—well…' His smile was both rueful and despairing. 'You can see the result.'

'The wound looks clean to me, and will probably heal in next to no time. Why don't you put your feet up on the couch, and I'll go and get a dustpan to clear up the broken glass?'

Flying down the corridor and then two flights of stairs to the kitchen, switching on all the lights as she went to illuminate her way, Marianne was back in the shortest time, noting with satisfaction that Eduardo had done as she'd requested and put his feet up. For the first time she realised that he was still wearing the clothes he'd had on during the day, although several of the buttons on the light blue shirt were casually undone, the formally smart black trousers were creased and his feet devoid of socks or shoes. Switching on another lamp that stood on the shelf of a nearby bookcase, she cleaned up the broken glass with long-practised efficiency, leaving the cleaning implements near the doorway to take away later. Then she returned to the silent male figure on the couch.

'I'd better take another look at that cut…just to make sure it's as clean as I first thought.'

Sitting down beside him, feeling her body grow warm at the contact with his—albeit out of *practical* necessity and not intimacy—Marianne efficiently re-examined the cut. Seeing to her satisfaction that all was well, she carefully bandaged the handkerchief round Eduardo's hand again, tying the ends into a firm knot to secure it.

'You'll live. It will throb a bit, that's all, and probably

won't even leave a scar. The lamp took the brunt of the damage, by the look of it. The fixing is all bent out of shape. Can it be rescued? It looks expensive.'

Sensing the man beside her tense even more, Marianne came face to face with his disparaging scowl.

'Do you think I care about what it is worth?'

She lifted her shoulders in a thoughtful shrug. 'To some people it might be a prized possession.'

'I do not have any "prized possessions", so you need not concern yourself about that!'

'All right, then...I won't. Shall I go and make you a hot drink? Some warm milk with some brandy in it, perhaps...? Something that might help you sleep?'

'You'd be wasting your time.'

'Why?'

'Only a miracle would help me sleep.'

'Still...it's better to try *something* than do nothing at all and resign yourself to the worst.'

'Marianne?'

'Yes?' By now she had risen to her feet, and as Eduardo's searing blue gaze examined her she was suddenly conscious that she stood before him in her dressing gown. It was a practical, no-nonsense kind of garment—neither pretty *nor* flattering—but still... Marianne was hardly immune to the intimate spell the night could cast, and beneath the soft dove-grey wool her body's long-suppressed need for touch was stirring vividly to life.

'You must think me extremely ill-mannered.' The

rich voice was slightly hoarse, as though he spoke over a throat that pained him. 'I did not thank you for helping me, and I want you to know that I am not ungrateful.'

'You're welcome. I would do the same for anybody.'

'And that very nicely puts me in my place, does it not?'

'What do you mean?'

'Your regard for my welfare is not particular…why should it be? It is merely a practical reaction on your part that you would employ with *anybody* in similar need. Tell me…has there ever been anyone in your life who *did* command your particular regard, Marianne?'

The man on the sofa studied her with such an expression of burning curiosity that she knew there was absolutely no possibility whatsoever of wriggling out of giving him an answer. Seriously troubled, Marianne struggled to summon the words that would reveal the truth of her past—the situation that she should have revealed to Eduardo from the moment he had offered her a job and a home but unfortunately had not…

CHAPTER SEVEN

MARIANNE'S clearly uncomfortable glance settled on the dying orange embers of the fire, and Eduardo saw her shiver.

'Shall I put some more coal on? It's grown a little chilly in here,' she said.

'*After* you have answered my question,' Eduardo said firmly. For some reason his heartbeat was accelerating a little at what she might be going to tell him. 'Shut the door,' he advised. 'Then you will not feel so cold.'

She did as he suggested, then stepped silently towards the fireplace. Thrusting out her hands, she stole whatever heat remained and then, wrapping her arms round her slim frame, said quietly, 'There was a man once that I cared about…we were married for less than a year.'

Married? He didn't echo the word out loud in astonishment or perhaps in *protest*, as his instinct dictated, but Eduardo felt it resonate through him like a thunderclap—a precursor to a storm of feelings and disturbances he hardly knew how to contain.

'It does not seem conceivable that you were married so young,' he commented instead. '*Too* young. What happened? Did you divorce?'

'No.' Turning her bewitchingly pretty face towards him, Marianne held Eduardo's gaze with resolute steadiness. 'He—he died.'

'Died?'

'Yes.'

'How?'

'A very rare form of cancer.' Her shoulders hunched.

Her ensuing sigh was as delicate as a newborn child's, yet he heard it just the same. Feeling genuine sympathy, Eduardo wanted to react appropriately, consolingly, but his feelings raised the familiar spectre of his own devastating loss, and he found himself staying where he was as if turned to stone, wondering how people bore the sometimes dreadful things that happened to them, where they found the strength. Then, knowing that he had failed miserably in that department because he had *not* found strength—it was shame and guilt and the need for self-punishment that made *him* endure, nothing noble at all—he clenched his jaw hard.

'Did he leave you with nothing?' he demanded, his words underscored with indignant anger on Marianne's behalf that her dying husband had clearly left her completely unprovided for. So much so that she'd had to resort to practically begging at the side of the road!

'What?' The question had clearly stunned her.

'Look at the situation he left you in! How long since he died?'

'Eighteen months.'

'And he left you completely without the means to support yourself?' Hearing the judgment and fury in his own voice, Eduardo made no apology for it.

'No… He left me his house and—and some money.'

Confusion taking over from rage, he glanced at Marianne in genuine surprise. 'So what happened? Why was it that I found you in the street busking? And in temperatures that would prevent most people from even going outside unless they absolutely *had* to, let alone stand there singing!'

'I was learning to perform in public, like I told you before. Music is a passion of mine and I wanted to get better at it. I thought I might eventually join a band or something, make my living that way. I was also trying to rebuild my confidence after what happened.'

'So you were not going home to some—some hostel or homeless shelter each night?'

'No. I'm sorry if I gave you that impression.'

'What happened to the house and the money you were left? Why phone me and tell me that you were in need of a job and home?'

Regarding Marianne's young, beautiful face, lit so beguilingly by the dying light of the fire, Eduardo couldn't deny the colossal disappointment and sense of betrayal that simmered inside him. What game was she playing that she would deceive him about her situation like this? Had she perhaps discovered who he was, learning that he had the kind of wealth that most people could only fantasise about? Perhaps her husband's modest legacy of money and a house were not *enough* for a secretly financially ambitious girl like her? The very idea turned his stomach.

'When I rang you and asked for your help it was because I truly needed it. I didn't lie about that.' She was twisting her hands round the belt of her robe, and her expression was genuinely in earnest, Eduardo saw. 'I needed a job and a home because—'

'Go on?'

'Because I gave the house and money and everything else that belonged to him to my husband's adult children.'

'Your husband had adult children?'

'Yes.'

'From that I gather that he was much older than you?'

'Yes. He was fifty-nine when we met.'

Moving away from the fire, Marianne turned her back on Eduardo for a moment. He saw the slender shoulders lift and then drop again, as though she was resigned to the fact that now she'd begun her story she would have to see it through to the end. As she turned back to face him, he detected the tiniest quiver of her lush top lip.

'He was a good man, and a kind one…a genuinely caring soul. Over a fairly short period of time we became great friends. After a while he asked me to marry him, and I agreed. When he left me the house in his will his children contested it, insisting that because he had been ill he couldn't have been in his right mind to do such a thing.' Her expression was anguished for a moment.

'I never asked Donal—my husband—to leave me anything. I'd made my own way before I met him and I would again. But he made me promise that I would hold onto the house so I would have some sense of security. Life was very difficult for a while after he went…dealing with grief and loss, I mean. The legal wrangles over the house made it even more challenging. I finally decided that I didn't want to be in a battle any more. More than anything I wanted peace. So I wrote to Michael and Victoria, his children, and told them they could have the house *and* the money. In the same letter I returned the keys. So you see…when I told you I needed a job and a home…it was perfectly true. I wanted to tell you before, but somehow it never seemed to be the appropriate time.'

Rubbing at his temples, Eduardo frowned. Not one in *ten* women would have done what Marianne had done—given away the house that was legally hers, leaving herself with nothing. He was sure of it. What would her husband have made of such a gesture? he mused, more disturbed than he cared to be at the thought of her being married to a man more than twice her age. More startling still was the idea that they had *both* lost their spouses. Both had experienced the numbing dark realm of bereavement. Although perhaps the expected loss of Marianne's husband due to his illness had been a little less hard to take than the shattering blow Eduardo had been dealt.

Not wanting to revisit such sombre recollections any more tonight, he suddenly realised that the woman in front of him displayed all the signs of being dead on her feet from fatigue—and he was the cause.

'Go to bed,' he told her curtly. 'You have an early start in the morning.'

'Please don't think I came here under false pretences…I would hate that. I'm not a liar. When you left me your card and told me if I ever changed my mind about needing a job and a home I should ring you, I took you at your word.'

'And I honoured my word, did I not? Now…you have done quite enough for one night, playing both nurse *and* housemaid, and you clearly need your sleep.'

'What about you?'

As Marianne stepped towards Eduardo her question was suspended on air that was subtly but exquisitely charged with an awareness that made his breath slow inside his chest and his mouth dry. He could not take his eyes off her. Her loveliness mesmerised him. With her long hair spilling over her shoulders like dark molten honey, her waist impossibly small, and her form so slender even in the unflattering dressing gown she was a sight that would make most men long to possess her. Silently he echoed that longing. But instead of surrendering to his great desire to hold her, instinctively Eduardo tensed. Desperately he wanted her to come closer, but at the same time the polar extremes of honour and self-loathing were causing him to contain his yearning and pray for it to dissipate.

'What *about* me?' he echoed, gravel-voiced.

'You need your sleep too. Please let me go and get you that hot drink or some brandy.'

'I have survived nights like these before *without* the need for hot drinks or brandy, and I will do so again. Please just do as I say and go back to bed.'

'All right, then—if you're sure?'

Deliberately not meeting her gaze, Eduardo glanced down at his neatly bandaged hand instead and said nothing.

Knowing that Eduardo's already sleepless night had been further disrupted by his accident, Marianne crept round the large, imposing house like a mouse, intent on doing her work as quietly as humanly possible so as not to disturb him. In the kitchen she played the radio at the lowest volume, and closed the door behind her as she prepared and chopped vegetables in readiness for yet another hearty soup for lunch. But occasionally during her work her gaze strayed out of the window to the alluring country views outside that made her heart leap with longing.

The Siberian winter was starting to abate at last, and everywhere there were signs that the deep snow was melting. Even as she stood by the sink, peeling carrots into a colander, Marianne heard the steady 'drip-drip' of icicles thawing under the eaves. She found herself speculating if Eduardo might invite her to take another walk with him. If he did, she wouldn't hesitate to say yes, she decided. Perhaps this time they might get a bit further than the little wooden bridge over the moat and head off into the forest that she was so longing to explore? The crisp, clean air as well as the exercise would definitely be beneficial.

What was it that troubled the man so deeply, seeming to steal away any pleasure he might find in simply being alive? she asked herself. She could understand a young, fit man like him being depressed about not being able to move as freely as he normally might because of his infirmity, but something told Marianne it wasn't just his limp that was causing him pain. Occasionally she had observed what she believed to be deep trauma in his arresting blue eyes, and it was starting to seriously disturb her. That, coupled with the lack of personal photographs or anything alluding to his past or where he came from in the house, as well as his propensity for being reclusive, and she was beginning to suspect something dreadful had happened to him…something so dreadful that even his valet Ricardo refused to be drawn about it.

And now there was another thing that bothered Marianne. Last night in the intimate confines of Eduardo's room, seeing the distress he'd fought so hard to hide from her and witnessing his pain, she had almost given in to her great desire to reach out and offer him much more *human* comfort. Holding his hand while she examined the cut he had sustained had been a test of endurance in more ways than one—especially when her hands had been trembling the entire time she tended his wound. She had never been so affected just by being *near* a man before…as though all this time her senses had been lying dormant and only now had come to life because *he* walked into a room.

The idea of being close to Eduardo plunged her into turmoil. She had certainly never experienced such wild, almost *painful* longing when she had been with dear Donal…but then they had never been intimate. His illness had simply prevented it. And after he had died Marianne had been glad they had not enjoyed true marital intimacy, because she had started to acknowledge that her feelings for him—although devoted—had in reality been only platonic.

Frowning at the guilt she'd suffered over that realisation, she reached out to straighten the little terracotta pot of fresh basil on the windowsill, almost jumping out of her skin when the door opened and Eduardo appeared.

'Good morning,' he greeted her, his expression disarmingly sheepish. 'Or perhaps I should say good afternoon? I did not realise I had slept in quite so late. You should have alerted me to the time.'

'I don't think so,' Marianne answered, hazel eyes widening in mild reproach. 'It seems to me that extra sleep was just what you needed! Why don't you sit down and I'll make you some coffee? Or if you'd prefer to go into the sitting room I'll bring it to you in there. I've lit the fire, so it's nice and warm.'

But Eduardo was already moving towards the big pine table in the centre of the stone-flagged floor. 'I think I will stay here with you,' he said, drawing out a chair and lowering himself into it. 'I am a little tired of my own company just now. The snow is starting to melt at last, I see.'

'I know. But it's still freezing outside.' Following the direction of his brooding gaze out of the window, Marianne kept her voice deliberately neutral, intuitively guessing that it was probably wise not to mention last night.

But then, just as she was about to fill the kettle with water, she glimpsed the reddened gash on his hand and realised he'd removed the makeshift bandage she'd made.

'How's that cut this morning?' she asked. 'I hope it wasn't too painful during the night?'

'It is nothing. I have already forgotten about it.'

'I'll check it again after you've had your coffee' Marianne said lightly, turning on the tap, filling the kettle and inserting the plug into the wall socket.

'There is no need for you to trouble yourself any further about it.'

Did he dislike the idea of her touching him? Marianne wondered. And she was unable to stem the hurt that thought produced.

'Well…perhaps you're ready for some breakfast, then? If you'd like something cooked it's no trouble.'

'No food. Just coffee.'

As if realising he had sounded a little curt, Eduardo

softened his reply with a smile. It was as though she'd been given the most monumental gift. Marianne sensed pleasure gush through her bloodstream like hot water springs, and to hide her burning cheeks she turned away to scoop pungent dark roasted coffee into the cafetière and place a matching cup and saucer on a tray.

'Marianne?'

'Yes?'

'I was thinking that maybe you'd agree to take a walk with me after I have had my coffee. Up towards the forest, perhaps?'

'Are you feeling up to going so far?'

Turning, she was just in time to catch Eduardo grimace, as if the last thing he wanted was to be reminded of his infirmity, and Marianne could have bitten out her tongue at her tactlessness.

'If I was not feeling up to it I would not have suggested it,' he replied, clearly attempting to quell any irritation inside him and making a deliberate effort to sound more agreeable instead.

'In that case, I'll be happy to go with you,' she told him, turning back to the kettle and pouring boiling water into the waiting cafetière…

In silence they made their way across the bridge, then onto the path that wound its way into the dense, still snow-covered forest. Now and again Marianne glanced to her side, to make sure Eduardo was not in difficulty, but she soon got the message that it would be unwise to display too much concern. Just a glimmer of a warning glance was all it took, so Marianne walked onwards without comment, her booted feet crunching on deep snow that was still treacherously slippery in places, the freezing air caressing her face with the cold kiss of winter at its deepest.

On either side of them tall trees rose up like dark walls hemming them in, and the path seemed to thin to a bare ribbon in places. She knew that, much as she might like to wander off at will, it would not be a good idea on a day with conditions as potentially treacherous as this. As soon as the lighter, milder days of spring arrived, then it would be an excursion to savour. *But would she still be here in the spring?* For that matter…would Eduardo?

Unable to hold back the fear that suddenly swarmed through her, Marianne stopped walking to study the silent, handsome man at her side.

'Please tell me what's wrong with you!' she burst out, emotion welling up inside her. 'I can't bear not to know.'

'Because of what happened to your husband you ask this?' Eduardo sighed heavily into the frigid air. 'I have not got a terminal illness, if that is what you are worried about.'

'Then what's wrong with your leg—and why do you so often seem to retreat where no one can reach you?'

'The first question I will answer… The second I cannot.'

Marianne waited, the cold at the tips of her gloved fingers feeling like sharpened steel teeth nipping her. She clapped them together to try and restore some warmth.

'I was involved in a car accident...a very bad one.' He stared at the ground for long seconds, a pulse throbbing visibly in the side of his cheek. 'That is how I injured my leg. I have had nine operations to try and mend the shattered bone, and from time to time the pain is excruciating.'

'I'm so sorry.'

'Don't be.' His jaw hardened, and the steely look that he sometimes wore crept back into the pale blue gaze now focused on Marianne. 'It was my own fault, and I must pay the price.'

'What are you saying?' She frowned. 'That you *deserve* the pain?'

'Now that you know I am not going to die any time soon, let us walk on or turn back.'

'Eduardo?'

'What is it?' His answering glance was predictably impatient.

'You are much too hard on yourself, I think.'

She knew she risked him telling her to mind her own business, but Marianne couldn't help herself. Once again he had gone to that place where no one could follow, and she longed to bring him back.

'Have you always spoken your mind so easily?' he asked.

To her surprise, when she glanced over she found Eduardo was smiling, and her stomach did a one-hundred-and-eighty-degree cartwheel. 'Not always. But it seems to me that people waste too much time pretending and not saying what they really feel.'

'You are probably right about that. Now have you had enough of an adventure for one afternoon? I think we should turn back, don't you? The sky is looking rather dismal and threatening.'

'I suppose we ought—'

Turning too suddenly, Marianne felt her booted foot slip on some ice, and the next thing she knew was she was lying flat on her back in the freezing snow, staring up at Eduardo as if he were a skyscraper above her.

'Marianne!' As he bent towards her, his expression was shocked and bleached of colour.

Inexplicably, laughter bubbled up inside her chest, her peal of mirth ringing out clearly as a bell in the still, silent forest, agitating some birds that were nesting in a nearby oak.

As they flew away, in a cacophony of flapping wings, Eduardo glanced back down at Marianne, his handsome face a picture of confusion and uncertainty. 'I do not see what is so funny,' he said gruffly. 'You might have hurt yourself badly! Do not try to get up too quickly. Here… let me help you.'

Allowing his cane to fall onto the ground, he put out both hands to aid Marianne, but even as she struggled to get to her feet again her humour did not dissipate.

'I didn't even hurt myself! That was what was so funny. I made a perfect landing…just like an acrobat or a prima ballerina!'

Her eyes damp with mirth, she was now upright, and her gaze locked with the man still holding her hands.

Seeing something there that made her heart stall, she felt her laughter die as abruptly as it had arisen.

'Do you have any idea how beautiful you are? How bewitching and lovely?' Eduardo murmured hoarsely. Then, urgently impelling her into his arms, he kissed her as though her lips were pure lifesaving oxygen…

CHAPTER EIGHT

AM I DREAMING? Can this really be happening to me?

As Eduardo held her and kissed her, Marianne forgot the piercing cold weather, also the fact that her jeans and jacket were now soaked and freezing from her graceful fall onto the snow, and instead clung to the steely warmth of his body coming through his cashmere coat, letting the intoxicating flavours and erotic taste of the man flood her senses. It was the first real passionate kiss she had ever had—a roaring fire in the midst of bitter winter—and she wanted it to last for ever…

But already Eduardo was lifting his lips away from hers—albeit reluctantly—cupping her face in his leather-gloved hands, staring deep into her eyes as though he could gaze and gaze at her and never get tired of the sight of her.

'Forgive me if that was a liberty I should not have taken,' he said huskily, and all Marianne could think was what incredibly long lashes he had, and how the little bump in the bridge of his nose was the perfect flaw in a face that would otherwise be almost *too* handsome and unforgettable for words. 'But I am not going to tell you I regret it,' he confessed, a corner of his sensuous mouth wryly lifting. 'Not when I thought I might *die* if I did not!'

Marianne blinked up at him in surprise, his words causing dizzying feelings of delight and pleasure to drench her like warm summer rain. 'It was a lovely kiss, Eduardo…and obviously something you are very good at!'

Hearing the unconstrained pleasure in her voice, she felt self-conscious heat rush into her face, suddenly afraid that he might think her reply too candid for comfort. *But then why should she act as if she regretted his kiss when she didn't?*

When Marianne would have torn her glance away, Eduardo held her chin fast with his fingers, his expression bemused. 'Your disarming honesty is very refreshing…not to mention ego-boosting! But such refreshing candour could get you into trouble, *namorada*…especially where men are concerned. Come, we will go back now. You are cold and damp from the snow, and you need to get out of those wet clothes into something warm.'

'You're right…it *is* cold.' Wrapping her arms round her middle, suddenly unable to stop the violent shivering that seized her, Marianne glanced shyly back at him. 'Being out in such weather has definitely been invigorating.'

'That is certainly *one* word for it,' Eduardo replied drolly, reaching down into the snow to retrieve his cane and then smiling inscrutably. 'Although I can think of many others equally descriptive!'

Returning to his rooms from the personal gymnasium he had had installed with the most up-to-date equipment available before he had even moved into the house, after a punishing hour of exercise on the treadmill, Eduardo strode into his luxurious bathroom and turned on the shower. His body was throbbing warmly from his activities—and miraculously he was hardly experiencing any pain at all, despite probably overdoing the exercise.

His footsteps stilled on the marble-tiled floor. The memory of the kiss he had stolen from Marianne in the forest suddenly drowned him in heat—heat definitely *not* aroused by punishing exercise. His senses were reacting as though she stood right in front of him *naked*, and in an instant he was aching and hungry, and needing her as he had never needed another woman before...not even his tragic Eliana. Touching his fingers to his mouth with something like wonder, Eduardo replayed the erotic sensation of her damp sweet lips against his, the taste of her exquisitely satin tongue, her arresting body pressed hard against him so that he felt every shapely contour even through her layers of winter clothing. *He cursed beneath his breath in pure frustration.*

Good God! He could hardly contain his need and his lust! But so many things about Marianne had got to him that day. Her laughter, for one... It had arrowed straight into his heart, dislodging something he'd forgotten he even possessed: the ability to experience pleasure. How long since he had expressed humour so unguardedly, basking in the warmth that resulted from it? He couldn't even recall such a time…it could have been *years* for all he knew. Then, when he had helped Marianne up from the snowy ground where she had fallen, her spontaneous delight had quite taken him aback. Seeing how beautiful her unfettered joy had rendered her, Eduardo had suddenly craved to be part of it…to taste genuine happiness and pleasure on his lips for once, instead of bitterness and sadness, to remember what it felt like to be really *alive* and not have every sense deadened by grief and regret.

The reality of how she had tasted had not disappointed either. Kissing her had been like devouring lush chocolate-covered cherries in a warm sensuous bath, and his desire had been explosive. So much so that his hands had ached to explore every lovely inch of her right there and then, in the middle of that freezing forest.

As he sensed what that inflammatory thought did to his body, he glanced wryly downwards. Then, lifting his head and staring unseeingly at the cloud of steam arising from the hot shower, he realised how much he liked having this mesmerising woman around…realised that if she was *not* around he might descend into even *worse* misery and despair. She was diverting his mind as well as arousing his lust, and had banished his sombre mood for the first time in ages.

Feeling something close to optimism—a notion that

had been a stranger to him for quite some time—he peeled off the black T-shirt and sweatpants he'd worn to exercise and stepped gratefully beneath the scalding spray of hot water.

Having changed into warmer clothes, deposited her snow-dampened jeans into the laundry basket and hung her wet jacket on a coat hanger in the airing cupboard, Marianne took a quick shower and then returned downstairs to start preparing the evening meal.

An hour later, having made a pot of tea, she took it upstairs to Eduardo's study. Knocking tentatively on the heavy oak door, she tried very hard to quell her nervousness. Still intoxicated by his kiss, she was seized by a new self-conscious shyness at the thought of being in his company again, and even though he'd told her he *hadn't* regretted kissing her, she couldn't help wondering if in the interim he'd reached a different conclusion.

'Yes!'

At Eduardo's behest, Marianne entered the room. He was seated at his desk, his computer turned off and his expression suggestive of someone deep in thought rather than immersed in work. She couldn't help but wonder what was preoccupying him.

'I thought you might like a cup of tea,' she offered tentatively, laying the small wooden tray down on a clear portion of the desk beside him.

'That was thoughtful…thank you. For someone raised on strong Brazilian coffee, I am becoming inordinately fond of the English habit of afternoon tea,' he remarked, his voice warm.

'I probably drink far too much of the stuff than is good for me, to be honest, but old habits die hard.' Forcing herself to meet his gaze, Marianne immediately scented the warm, clean, definitely *erotic* smell of sandalwood soap that clung to him. There were other things she couldn't help noticing. The dark blond hair that was obviously still damp from his recent shower. The fresh white cotton shirt, and the jeans that looked as if they had been tailor-made for his hard lean body. The fact that he had also had a shave. There was a tiny spot of dried blood on his firm jawbone to confirm it.

'Marianne?'

'Yes?'

'You are staring at me.'

'Sorry...I was miles away.' Flustered, she turned away.

As she reached for the teapot to pour the tea, Eduardo caught her by the wrist and tugged her towards him. Finding herself precariously balanced against the steely wall of his chest, her jean-clad thighs trapped firmly between his as he held both wrists fast, she felt her heart thump so hard that she honestly feared she might faint.

'What are you—? What are you doing?'

'I am repaying the compliment,' he answered, an enigmatic little smile playing round his lips. 'Now I am staring at *you*.'

Saying no more, Eduardo freed her wrists, then

started to unbutton the shapeless red white and blue patterned cardigan she wore.

'Now what are you doing?' she asked nervously. The touch of his strong muscled thighs in the tough denim of his jeans was all but *burning* her skin through the slightly flimsier, cheaper material of her own.

'I want to take this off so that I can see properly how you are made. You seem to persist in wearing clothes that completely conceal your figure, and I do not understand it. Ah...*much* better. You are exquisite, *namorada*... quite exquisite. Such a tiny waist, and yet such perfect womanly hips too.'

All Marianne wore underneath the over-large sweater was a thin white T-shirt. Beneath that she was braless. Remembering the fact, she sensed her nipples all but drill holes in the skimpy material as Eduardo's sensual blue eyes lazily but thoroughly examined her figure. Then, without warning, he placed his hands either side of her hips and pressed her towards him. Just as she registered this, her lips collided with his, and his tongue thrust hungrily into her mouth, laying erotic claim to hers.

She heard the ravenous husky moan that escaped her, hardly recognising it as her own. But then even her *mind* seemed not to belong to her any more. It hovered, suspended in a whole other intoxicating hemisphere, as time and again wave upon wave of the most deliciously urgent sensations of pleasure, lust and need powerfully rocked through her body—feelings that up until now Marianne had had very little experience of.

Sliding his hands beneath her T-shirt, Eduardo cupped and stroked her breasts, inflaming her already aching, tingling nipples into stinging, hardened buds. Then he put his mouth to each breast in turn, at precisely the moment when Marianne believed she couldn't stand it any longer if he *didn't*, and suckled hard. Biting her lip, she instinctively and greedily held his head to her, sliding her fingers through the damp silky strands of his dark wheat hair as even more ragged moans of pleasure and want left her lips. The tight, clenched feeling deep in her womb practically *begged* for some way to be released. *Was this what she had been missing all this time, denying herself the physical intimacy and pleasure of being with a man?*

Immediately the question arose, Marianne knew it was only *this* man who was capable of arousing such wild abandon in her.

Lifting his head with a look that was both pleasurably sated as well as hungry for more, Eduardo readjusted her dishevelled clothing and rose slowly to his feet. 'I have a question for you.'

He locked his arms round her waist, and Marianne stared up at him as if in a dream. Yet she was fully and shockingly aware of the barely civilized, almost *feral* state of arousal reflected back at her from those haunting blue eyes. It was all she could do to keep breathing, never mind hope to answer him.

'If I asked you to come to me tonight and share my bed…would you?'

Deciphering her thoughts above the roar of rushing blood inside her head was a challenge. But even though Marianne's body was definitely *not* conflicted about what it needed, she still found herself hesitating. Feeling her fingers curl into the side of Eduardo's lean, hard waist, she breathed softly, 'Can we wait a little while before that happens? It's not that I don't want to, it's just that—'

'It is too soon for you? Of course. I understand.'

Gently he put her from him, and Marianne wasn't prepared for how cold she suddenly felt without him.

He continued, 'It's just that you arouse feelings in me that I haven't experienced for quite some time, and they are a little…' he grinned '…overwhelming.'

'You too have aroused similar feelings in me, Eduardo…strong feelings. But perhaps we could just spend an evening together instead? Maybe get to know each other a little better?' she suggested, heart thudding in case he refused.

Spying a chessboard on the middle shelf of a bookcase, she felt an idea start to form itself in her mind.

'Doing what? It would have to be something in which I would not constantly be distracted by you and want to touch you!' Eduardo admitted with a wolfish grin.

Sensing her whole body glow with pleasure, Marianne smiled. 'I see you have a chessboard…do you play?'

'Does it rain in the Amazon?'

Folding his muscular arms across his chest, he chuckled. He had the most mischievous look on his face that she had ever seen, and it made her tummy imitate the motion of a yo-yo.

'What are you suggesting? That we spend the evening playing chess? You think you can keep me occupied with your game for long enough so that we won't have to find something else to do?'

'Wait and see. I might just surprise you!'

'*Namorado*...you have already surprised me more than I ever could have believed possible.'

Looking as if he would once again draw her into his arms, Eduardo dropped his hands to his hips as if to regretfully contain the urge. Marianne chose that same moment to head for the door.

'It's a deal, then. I'll see you later,' she told him shyly as she let herself out.

Eduardo discovered that amongst the things he was starting to love about Marianne was one of the most relatively innocuous things of all: *watching her concentrate*. Many times during their now nearly four-hour chess game he had seen her exhibit myriad different expressions—sighs, pouts, chewing of the lips and thumbnails. His favourite was the way that little crease would appear in the flawless skin between her brows—usually just before she had achieved a move with the most lethal result—before relaxing again as though it had never been.

Having always loved the game, Eduardo had thought of himself as a fairly accomplished player—but after four hours of battling it out with Marianne she was beating him hollow. And the most surprising thing of all was that he didn't even *care*. Playing the ultimate game of strategy with his engaging companion had been so fascinating, so absorbing and enjoyable, that he had simply forgotten about everything else and relaxed. So much so that she had just declared checkmate.

'You've got a killer instinct.'

'Are you upset that I won?'

'Not at all. You were at least a couple of moves ahead of me every time. Watching you play was like observing a general conducting a military campaign! Who would have thought that behind those pretty quixotic eyes lurks such a calculatingly organised mind? You deserved to win. Who taught you to play so well?'

'My husband…we spent many hours playing when he was confined to bed because of his illness.'

Those two words 'husband' and 'bed' were enough to deflate Eduardo's newfound good humour as emphatically as a bucket of ice water poured over his head.

'You said he was much older than you?' he murmured, his glance flicking jealously over her lovely features in the glow of the firelight.

'Yes…he was fifty-nine. I told you.'

'So…you like older men as opposed to younger ones?'

She laughed, and the sound made heat radiate down his spine all the way to the tips of his fingers and toes. Just as if the touch of an angel had transfixed him.

'Age doesn't come into it if you like someone. It's the person I'm interested in…not what age they are or what they do or anything like that. It's not about ticking boxes, as some of those silly magazines would have you believe!'

'Hmm…'

'What does that mean…*hmm*?'

She gave him a look a mother might give to a recalcitrant child when she was trying to coax him into better behaviour, and Eduardo was amazed to realise that he felt almost *desperate* for her approval and attention. *What was happening to him?* He wanted to bed her. He knew that. But after what she had said earlier, when she'd asked if they could wait a while, he did not want to use his powers of seduction to persuade her against her will. Even so, not being able to have her was agonising.

'It means that tomorrow night I will beat you hollow when we play again!' he said irritably, and stood up.

Marianne too got to her feet, her face wreathed in the biggest smile. 'So you *did* mind me winning?'

'Not at all…I would just like the opportunity to even the score, that is all.'

'Fair enough.' As though completely unaware of the profound ache she'd inflicted on him—an incessant sensual need that Eduardo had been only too aware of all the time they'd been playing, which had not been helped by those breathy little sighs and unknowingly alluring pouts she'd been exhibiting all evening—Marianne rubbed her hand across her eyes and yawned.

'I think tiredness has finally caught up with me. I need my bed. Shall I put out the fire before I go?'

'Leave it,' he replied tersely, and then, immediately realising he sounded like a wounded bear, somehow found a smile for her. 'Go to bed. I will see to the fire. Goodnight, Marianne.'

'Goodnight, Eduardo.'

A quizzical little glance, a smile, and then she was gone…

Marianne had never guessed that the supposedly simple game of chess, played three absorbing nights in a row, could turn into an altogether *different* kind of battle. After practically every move each of them made on the chessboard their eyes would be instantly drawn to each other, and the tension that built between them would flare hotter and tighter, until she thought she might have to give in and *beg* Eduardo out loud to forget the mental battle of wills required by the game and take her to bed instead. But Marianne stuck to her restraint, her only consolation being that her partner was clearly suffering equally—if not *more*.

She could tell because, although he did not express his frustration out loud, his temper nearly got the better of him on a couple of occasions when he made the wrong move and Marianne bested him. She knew that wasn't the only reason he almost exploded. But the following day Ricardo was due to return, and once the other man was around it was inevitable the dynamics in the house would change. That being the case, she wondered if there would be any more evenings of companionable chess-playing—or would Eduardo revert back to the taciturn, wounded individual he'd been when she'd first moved into his house?

She prayed not. These past few evenings together she had discovered a humorous, playful side to him that warmed her heart—an aspect of his personality that she wanted to discover more of, not *less*. And it had made her start to believe that perhaps he was healing from the trauma of his accident at last.

'You know this has been an exercise in pure torture?' he announced now, as Marianne got up from her chair at the conclusion of their game—a game that Eduardo had won—and yawned and stretched.

She threaded her fingers through her recently shampooed hair and smiled. 'Because I put up such a fight and you didn't win easily?' she teased.

Her companion scowled. 'You know damn well that is not what I meant at all!'

He swore softly, momentarily turning away, as if to try and regain some composure. He turned back, and the longing and pure frustration etched in the chiselled contours of his handsome face almost made Marianne's knees buckle.

'I want you to come to me tonight,' he ground out hoarsely. 'Tell me that you will.'

She swallowed hard, her heart pounding. 'Yes, I'll come to you.' Her voice almost cracked at the tide of yearning that submerged her…

* * *

Having showered and put on her nightclothes, Marianne lay on top of the bed to read a little, in a bid to compose herself. It wasn't working. Finally giving up her futile attempt to comprehend anything on the page she was looking at, she put down the book, pushed aside the duvet she'd tucked her feet under, and left the bed. The night was cool, but her skin was almost too hot to bear. Dressed in one of the long white Victorian-style nightgowns she wore in winter for warmth, she moved gracefully across the floor to the window. The polished boards creaked a little beneath her light footsteps and sounded almost obscenely loud in the otherwise silent room.

Tonight the moon was half in shadow, and the light that filtered into her bedroom was muted and delicate. Moonlight, with its ethereal dependable presence, was sometimes a strange kind of comfort to her, but not tonight. Tonight, anticipating her promised visit to Eduardo's room, her every nerve was jangled, every feeling she possessed heightened to an almost unbearable degree. Everything had felt so…so *right* when he had kissed and touched her so satisfyingly in his study a few days ago—as if this ultimate intimacy would be utterly delightful and easy…wonderful, even… And night after night, as they'd duelled over their games of chess, the need inside her to have him hold her and love her had been building and building, until she thought she might well lose her sanity if it didn't happen soon.

Yet Marianne couldn't help apprehensively dwelling on one point in particular. What would Eduardo think when he found out her secret—the fact that she had never been with a man before—was still untouched even after six months of marriage? If he was looking for the kind of sexual satisfaction he had perhaps been used to then maybe he wouldn't be so keen to take her to bed after all. He might think her inexperience prevented that. If that turned out to be the case then how would she deal with the embarrassment and humiliation? Not to mention the *frustration* that was bound to follow his rejection of her?

CHAPTER NINE

SHE had made up her mind to tell Eduardo that she would decline his offer to share his bed. Too fearful of being rejected once he knew the truth, Marianne had told herself it was the best decision. Besides, she argued, as she nervously ascended the staircase to the upper floor, the flickering up-lighters casting her slim shadow on the walls as she moved, she hadn't come here to have an affair with Eduardo. He had given her a job and a home for however long she wished, and they were becoming friends. She would not compromise her position *or* his by sleeping with him. No matter *how* much the idea tempted her.

But when he opened the door to her tentative knock, standing before her in navy silk pyjama bottoms and nothing else, Marianne's carefully rehearsed explanation and sensible resolve disappeared quicker than ice on a barbecue. Her throat drying, all she could do was stare at the totally animal and totally sexy specimen of masculinity that confronted her as if she'd been struck dumb. In turn, Eduardo's slow measuring gaze silently appraised her, in the hastily donned robe she'd thrown on over her Victorian nightgown, a definite glint of amusement in the pastel blue depths.

'I've been waiting for you,' he said finally, the velvet burr of his rich voice raising all the hairs on the back of her neck. 'Come in.'

'I was—'

'Yes?'

When she still didn't move, Eduardo took her by the hand to draw her into the room. Two small ornate lamps glowed softly, lending intimate warmth to the opulent surroundings and rendering areas of the room to mysterious shadow. Daring a longer glance over Eduardo's hard-muscled shoulder, Marianne saw that his bedroom door was ajar. Her heart all but climbed into her throat. Shutting the door firmly behind them, her companion slowly turned to survey her. A warm, earthy scent with undertones of a woody and masculine soap clung hypnotically in the air between them. He smiled at her. But it was all Marianne could do to tear her gaze away from the display of formidable muscle in the broad tanned chest that was dusted with darkly golden hair—a sight that made her feel as if she'd just imbibed a shot of strong whisky that had gone straight to her head.

'You were saying?' Eduardo teased, and before she had a chance to reply tilted her chin towards him to claim her already quivering lips in the softest, yet most earth-shattering of gentle kisses.

'I—I forget what I'm thinking when you do things like that,' Marianne admitted breathlessly, her legs trembling hard beneath her nightclothes.

'You too make me forget everything when I look into your eyes.' He smiled. Catching her hand again, he led her towards the open bedroom door. 'You must be one of the few women in the world able to get away with something like this,' he was saying as they stood beside a huge canopied bed that Marianne was certain wouldn't look out of place in one of the royal palaces.

'Get away with what?' she asked, hazel eyes round with alarm.

'This—this virginal but very sexy and alluring nightgown.' He collected a soft swathe in his hand to study it.

With the unknowingly apt comment echoing in her ears, Marianne was too frozen to move for a moment, and she watched him lean towards her to ease her robe from her shoulders in silence, just as if she was one of those mythical creatures from an old folk tale, turned to stone after helplessly glancing at something forbidden. The garment slithered to the floor in a whisper-soft rustle that was still too loud to her heightened sense of hearing, and it snapped her out of the trance she'd fallen into—only for her to become shockingly aware that the tiny teardrop pearl buttons on the bodice of her nightgown were being carefully unhooked one by one by the man in front of her.

His glance was focused and intent, as if he were anticipating revealing something wondrous, and Eduardo didn't utter a single word as he undertook this task. Trembling reaction set in, and Marianne feverishly wondered what had happened to her resolve to decline sharing his bed tonight. Try as she might, she knew she didn't have a hope of resurrecting it…not with the irresistibly seductive way this man so effortlessly commanded her mind, body and attention as he was doing right now. Yet she couldn't totally allow herself to be swept away by his expert seduction. *Not yet.*

As he undid the last button in the long row on her bodice, then pushed the material aside to reveal a smooth pale shoulder along with a generous glimpse of breast, Marianne clamped an anxious slender hand over his much larger one.

'Eduardo…' A helpless tremor seized her voice. 'There's something I should tell you.'

A tiny crease appeared between his dark blond brows, his expression reflecting both mild concern and gentle amusement. 'What is it, little one? You are not going to tell me that you are suddenly feeling nervous?'

'If I'm nervous it's because I have—I have cause to be. I've never—that is to say—' Her gaze shied away from his as she struggled to articulate words that lodged uncomfortably in her throat. 'I've never been with a man before…'

Letting go of Eduardo's hand, she curled a few long strands of honey-coloured hair round her ear, chewing heavily down on her lip at the same time.

'All the way, I mean…'

At first he looked stunned. Then a dark shadow of fury passed across the compelling contours of his handsome face.

Gathering the two sides of her gown protectively across her breasts, Marianne automatically stepped back.

'How can that be when you told me you were married? Was that a *lie*?' he demanded.

'No…it wasn't a lie. But Donal—my husband—he was ill when we married, and it just wasn't possible for him to—for us—' Feeling her face flame scarlet at having to reveal something of such a painfully intimate nature to the man standing before her, Marianne moved her head in a gesture of despair.

'You are telling me that the marriage was never consummated?'

'Yes, I am.'

He said something in Portugese that she was sure must mean *unbelievable*.

'And you never had an intimate relationship with a man before you married?'

'No.'

A spark of indignation surfaced inside her that Eduardo was quizzing her like this—that he might think her strange or odd for not having slept with a man before—and her fear of being rejected by him made her want to run away before he got the chance to do it.

'Do you have any more questions? If you're finished acting as some kind of inquisitor then I think I'll go back to my room!'

'Marianne?'

Unbelievably his hand was sliding round her jaw, tipping her face towards him. He was definitely *not* behaving like a man about to reject her, she saw, and her heart began to race.

'I am sorry that you were denied the pleasure and comfort of intimacy with your husband…but I am *honoured* that you would consider giving this great gift to me.'

'You—you still want me?' Her voice dropped to a hoarse whisper.

'More than ever.'

He demonstrated the fact by claiming her mouth in a kiss that was so voracious and commanding Marianne thought her already weakened limbs might fold beneath her like some delicate piece of origami. Yet underlying the sensuous caress the feeling persisted in her that there was a measure of distinct control there too—as if he didn't want to scare or overwhelm her. Surely it was *rare* to meet a man so mindful of a woman's sensitivity that he would curtail the strength of his own desire in deference to her inexperience? She could only conclude that Eduardo De Souza was a man in a million.

But secretly she *wanted* him to lose control with her, she realised. She was certain that she could match his passion, and give him pleasure too…the pleasure he inexplicably so often seemed to deny himself.

Withdrawing her lips from his, Marianne studied him longingly from beneath her lashes. 'I want you too,

Eduardo, so you don't have to treat me as if I'm made of glass. I know that whatever happens you won't hurt me.'

Even as the shy confession left her lips her blood was pounding with a primal yearning to be even closer to him. Everything about this man seemed to inflame her, making her behave in a way that was quite unlike her normal self. He growled and pulled her hard against him. Sighing, Marianne wound her arms round his neck to steady herself. Engulfed by heat and longing, she knew there was not one inch of her entire body where Eduardo's kisses or touch would not be an utter delight to her.

She'd been alone for too long, and silently she admitted that she had a great need to be held, touched, tasted, even driven a little crazy by a lover…someone who would help her forget her painful past and make her think only of today instead.

Now, coming into contact with the intimate caress of the proud male erection beneath the smooth silk of his pyjamas, Marianne found her hips impelled hard against Eduardo's, so that she was left in no doubt as to the extent of his desire for her. His hands shaped her body through the material of her gown, following every line of every curve as though it were imperative he discovered every part of her.

Riveted by the feverish bolt of desire that surged through her, Marianne became aware that the edge of the bed was only bare inches away. The room seemed to spin dizzyingly for a moment as Eduardo guided her back against it, his touch gentle yet commanding.

'I want this first time to be unforgettable for you, *namorada...*' His eyes darkened with feeling. 'All you have to do is lie still and let me pleasure you.'

Gathering the smooth crisp cotton of her nightgown as she sat on the bed, he lifted it over her head and discarded it. Marianne's long rippling hair fell in a honey-coloured cloud round her bare shoulders and gooseflesh chased across her skin as the cool night air hit her. She saw the appreciative gleam in Eduardo's avid gaze as his glance travelled slowly up and down her body, and now it wasn't just the cool air that made her shiver.

'You are even more beautiful in the flesh than I imagined,' he murmured softly, catching silken strands of her hair between his fingers and examining them. 'Bewitchingly so. There is not a man in the world who would not *envy* me right now.'

Letting go of her hair, he tipped her back onto the bed so that she was lying supine and positioned himself above her. The most libidinous smile hijacked his mouth. Marianne sighed. The sensation of his hard and heavy male body against hers was blissfully delicious as he carefully closed the gap between them. *He was all she could have dreamed of and more*, she thought eagerly. The lightly tanned skin that encased his strong fit muscles was smooth as silk and warming as cashmere—and the way he looked at her...the way he looked at her made her feel as if she was some irresistible edible delight he simply *had* to have, and the only woman in the world he had ever gazed at in that way.

Even knowing that that couldn't possibly be true didn't lessen her enjoyment.

'Close your eyes' he ordered, bending his head towards her.

Her lids obediently shut, she felt Eduardo's slow devastating kiss melt her to her very core. It was as though she were a sensual swirling river being caressed by living, breathing sunlight. A sense of aliveness and vitality transfixed her, making her feel desired and wanted beyond belief. In her womb, a tight, hot, coiled sensation was growing.

Uninhibitedly returning his kiss, eagerly absorbing and tasting unique and intoxicating male flavours that she could never imagine tiring of, Marianne wondered how she had never guessed making love could be this sublime. Her slender thighs moved restlessly against Eduardo's hipbones, her body willing him to claim what she was now *more* than ready to give him. But still he took his time with her, caressing her and taking the sensitive tips of her breasts deep into the warm velvet cavern of his mouth. His teeth and tongue tasted and teased until she seriously thought she would explode with the sheer sensual euphoria of it.

Mindless with need now, Marianne pushed her fingers hungrily through his hair, wanting and needing to touch and feel every part of him, vowing to memorise every moment, every electrifying detail, so that she would never forget it. Moving her hands down to Eduardo's iron-hard broad shoulders, she sensed the sheathed muscle and bone there with deeply primal satisfaction. He was surely the living embodiment of the kind of man a woman fantasised about in her most private dreams, she mused. Whenever she'd allowed herself to dream of a man making love to her—the way he was made, how he looked, how he tasted—the reality of *this* man was what she'd secretly ached for, she realised. He was just perfect in every way. There was no conflict in her mind about giving the gift of her virginity to him. And afterwards there would be no regrets, she assured herself. Not now…not *ever*.

Lifting his head, Eduardo kissed her on the lips once more, his tongue thrusting with avid hunger inside her mouth, stroking over the velvet and satin textures with expert erotic thoroughness before moving down her body once again—this time making a sizzling damp trail slowly and devastatingly across her ribcage. Reaching her waist, the silken glide of his warm tongue intimately acquainted itself with her navel. Marianne shivered. Increasing her torment, he moved lower still.

Finally, at the shockingly erotic sensation of his mouth and tongue laving at her most deeply feminine centre, she writhed in thrilling ecstasy, biting her lip and curling her fingers into the luxurious counterpane covering the bed as the almost unbearable tension inexorably building inside her finally surrendered to the bliss that promised to follow.

Nothing could have prepared her for the full extent of those incredible moments. Intense waves of stunning sensation washed over her again and again, and suddenly, helplessly, shockingly, her eyes were awash with tears. She had never experienced such utter vulnerability yet such incredible connection with someone before, and it shook her to her very soul.

'Eduardo…' Her voice thick with emotion, she uttered his name. His dazed, aroused gaze seared her with palpable heat as he rose to join her. With an awed look Marianne placed her hands either side of the stunning masculine face that she knew would be imprinted on her heart and mind for ever. 'That was wonderful.'

'It was my pleasure.'

'What can I— How can I—? I mean, now I want to make *you* feel good too.'

He chuckled softly. 'Believe me, my angel, I have not felt this good in a long, long time! But do not worry… we are not finished yet.'

Although his glance was wry, there was deep purpose in it. Sitting back a little, he started to ease the navy silk pyjama pants he still wore down over his arrow-straight hips.

Watching him, Marianne felt her mouth go dry. It was a revelation to her that a woman could lust after a man with the same fervent desire with which a man could want a woman. But suddenly she remembered his injured leg and, concerned that he might be in pain and keeping it from her, she frowned and leaned towards him, her intention to assist him in whatever way she could.

'Be careful!' she entreated as she saw him briefly

wince. But never had a man wanted help *less* than Eduardo did right then, she saw. His look no longer wry, he threw her a brief hard glare. 'I invited you to my room to be my lover tonight…not my nurse! I am no invalid who needs your care and attention as your husband did!'

Stung by the harshness of his reply, Marianne felt her cheeks burn hotly. 'Why do you have to be like this?' She made a little motion of despair with her hands. 'I know very well you're not an invalid. You're—you're everything I ever dreamt a lover would be, Eduardo.'

'Then come over here.'

She didn't even have a moment's hesitation. Her body was still filled with languorous heat from his lovemaking, and she had a great need to give him pleasure too. She knew that that was her genuine desire, so his huskily voiced command could do nothing but thrill her.

He tipped up her chin. 'I did not mean to scold you,' he said gruffly. 'Sometimes I just react too quickly. Perhaps you would like to help me in another way?'

The glimpse of despair she'd seen in his haunting blue eyes had now been replaced by a spine-tingling boyish grin, and Marianne saw that he was opening a small foil packet and extracting the contents. Her heart skipped a beat as he looked her straight in the eyes.

'I know you have never done this before, but I will guide you if you like.'

'All right.' Her voice had dropped to half its normal strength.

Revealing himself in all his magnificent glory,

Eduardo guided her hands to the latex protection and helped her sheathe him. Touching and seeing him like this, feeling the silky hardness and the heat that radiated so powerfully beneath her fingers, Marianne couldn't help but tremble. Inside, a tumult of feelings flooded her. Yes, she was nervous—but she was undeniably excited too. *She was also a little concerned that there might be some pain.* Above all she was grateful that her lover had thought about the practicalities of the situation—because, to her shame, *she* hadn't.

'It will be all right *namorada*…trust me,' Eduardo soothed. 'I will be as gentle as I can.'

Sitting astride her hips, he bent his head to claim another passionate, hungry kiss. The harsh graze of the stubble round his jaw scratched her a little, but Marianne didn't care. Lost in the sheer enjoyment of what was happening, she jerked as she sensed Eduardo's hands firmly guiding her slender thighs apart and his fingers probing her. Scalding heat rushed straight to her core and she couldn't help the sensual little moan that was breathlessly ejected from her lips. Her own dampness and readiness stunned her, and now her thighs parted of their own hungry volition to invite the ultimate attention from her lover.

Eduardo's aroused sex explored her tentatively at first. Then, seeing how ready she was, he pressed into her more firmly. Marianne shut her eyes to absorb the unfamiliar sensation of penetration. There was a momentary feeling of stinging discomfort followed by a sense of voluptuous fullness. Then, as he started to move more easily and rhythmically inside her, she relaxed, surrendering totally to the pleasure that was filling her.

Pale blue eyes had now darkened to cobalt, focused fixedly on her face, and Eduardo's incredible body was seized by one consuming purpose. Once more tension built inside her, and Marianne anchored her hands on his tight bulging biceps as he thrust into her again and again, until all thoughts were swept away on a stunning erotic tide that lapped forcefully through her as if it would never cease. She must have cried out, because when she did the man above her stilled for a moment, then pierced the now musky air with a deep, guttural groan of his own. A thin sheen of sweat glistened on his brow and shoulders, and his mouth curved in a sensuous smile.

'I think I was just in paradise,' he told her, a husky catch in his voice.

Carefully lowering himself, he kissed Marianne full on the mouth again. There was such sweetness in his kiss that tears surged into her eyes. Blinking them away with a shy smile, she saw as Eduardo raised his head to study her that there was a concerned look on his face.

Brushing away the trail of moisture from her cheeks with the pad of his thumb, he stroked his fingers through her hair and frowned. 'I hope I was gentle enough for your first time and did not cause you pain?'

'I don't know why I cried. It wasn't because you hurt me Eduardo. I just feel a little emotional right now.'

'Then let us get into bed together and I will help you

relax. I will hold you in my arms all night, if you wish, and you can fall asleep there.'

'Are you sure? That you want me to spend the night with you, I mean?'

'Of course! Did you think I would send you from me so soon?'

'What about Ricardo?' Marianne asked, suddenly remembering that Eduardo's valet was due back from his trip the next day.

'What about him?' A dark blond eyebrow lifted quizzically.

'What if he sees me coming out of your room in the morning?'

Eduardo shrugged, clearly dismissing her concern. 'If he did he would not even comment on the fact. I can totally depend upon him to be discreet, so do not worry.'

'If you say so.'

'I do say so. Now, come and get into bed and stop searching for problems where none exist!'

He grinned disarmingly, and Marianne's heart turned over because in that moment he looked happier than she had ever seen him…

CHAPTER TEN

EDUARDO woke, astounded to find daylight pouring into the room. Realising that he had more or less slept through the whole night, apart from once drowsily opening his eyes to make sure that Marianne was still sleeping beside him, he could hardly believe what had occurred. Moving a little to test his limbs, he realised that there was very little discomfort or pain to be found anywhere. The knowledge amazed him. Instead of hurting, his body felt rested and replenished.

Contemplating the reason for this miracle, Eduardo turned on his side, propping himself up on his elbow to study the slumbering and enticing slender form next to him. His heart seemed to miss a beat. Even with the full glare of the morning sun exposing every feature and hiding nothing she was simply *ravishing*. How could she not be, with skin as smooth and unblemished as the most perfect peach, and her honey-coloured hair softly framing her face to fall gently over her shoulders in a silken tangle? Such a sight to start the day would surely make *any* red-blooded male rejoice. Once again Eduardo mentally framed the picture she made, knowing without conceit that if he were to shoot it, it would be much coveted by all who saw it.

But of course if he were to take Marianne's picture he would never consider selling the result or giving it away. *He would keep it for his own private delectation.* An almost irresistible urge gripped him to go and find his camera—a top-of-the-line professional Nikon, the one he had hidden away in the trunks that contained his belongings from Brazil. No matter how much he tried to tell himself that it was part of his old life, not the present—that it was probably best to just leave it alone, as he had vowed—as he rested his glance on Marianne Eduardo was not quite convinced that he should *keep* that vow after all. Smiling as he recalled how willingly and passionately she had surrendered the astonishing gift of her virginity to him last night, he sensed his blood heat, and slumbering desire stirred to commanding, aching life as he continued to appraise her.

'What's the time?' As if sensing his observation, Marianne opened her eyes. A cornucopia of dazzling green and gold dazzled him.

'Who knows? Does it matter?' Shrugging, Eduardo stroked his fingers gently down her flushed cheek.

'Of course it matters! I have to go back to my room and get ready for the day.' Pushing herself upright, Marianne swept back her hair with her hand, her anxious glance seeking out her scattered nightwear. 'It must be at least eight or eight-thirty, and I have to make breakfast and light the fires or the house will be stone-cold. Oh, Eduardo! Why didn't you wake me?'

'I did not want to disturb you because you looked so peaceful and beautiful lying there, my angel…like Sleeping Beauty herself. Can I be blamed for simply wanting to gaze at you?'

'But I'm not Sleeping Beauty, am I? In case you've forgotten, I'm your housekeeper—and I've got work to do.'

Her grumpy response to his compliment merely amused Eduardo. He would forgive her just about *anything* today after the pleasure they had shared last night. Spying her nightgown at the end of the bed, Marianne reached forward to grab it, yanking it unceremoniously down over her head—but not before Eduardo had a very edifying glimpse of her perfect blush-pink tip-tilted breasts and hourglass waist. He sat up, his arms possessively circling that lovely waist. Kissing the back of her head, he let the amber scent of her shampoo fill his nostrils even as her silken flowing hair tickled his nose.

'You do not have to work today. I am giving you the day off,' he told her.

Marianne jerked her head round in astonishment. 'That's all well and good, but—'

'What?'

'You can't just give me the day off like that when there's work that needs to be done! You need a housekeeper, Eduardo, and may I remind you that's why you hired me?'

'Housekeeper or no, what I need right now is *you*, here in my bed.'

Eduardo was sure desire thickened his voice and blazed from his eyes, and he made no attempt to disguise it—because as well as feeling aroused beyond measure, a great need had arisen inside him to be totally frank with this lovely woman.

'I've just realised something.' A dawning look stole over her face.

'What?'

As she twisted round in the bed so that she was facing him properly, Marianne's glance was one of joy and wonder. 'You slept right through! You didn't wake once…or at least if you did I didn't hear you. Did you wake? Did the pain in your leg disturb you?'

Grinning, Eduardo tenderly framed Marianne's face with his hands. 'It is perfectly true. I *did* sleep through the night. I woke just once—not because I was in pain, but just to make sure you were still there beside me, *namorada*.'

'I promised you that I'd stay,' she answered shyly, her gaze momentarily lowering. 'And I'm so glad you weren't in any pain. You've endured so much, coming through nine operations. You surely deserve some relief.'

'It has not been an easy time, for sure.'

'It must have been the most dreadful accident.'

Slowly Eduardo withdrew his hands from Marianne's face. He had no desire to ruin what had started out as a beautiful morning by confronting the terrible event that still haunted him and had left him a near cripple—yet he had made a vow to himself to be totally frank with Marianne. After the gift she had given him last night, she at least deserved to know how he had sustained his injury.

'It was. The worst day of my life.' He winced.

'Will you—can you tell me about it?' she probed gently.

He nodded. 'Yes—I will tell you.' Reaching for Marianne's hand, he examined it for a moment before continuing. 'It was late at night, and we were returning home from a party.'

'We…?'

Meeting her speculative glance, Eduardo steeled himself. Her sultry warm scent penetrated the air around him just then, and he almost suggested they forgot about the past and just enjoyed what they had right now. *But to his credit he did not.* With new resolve, he carried on relating the story.

'My wife Eliana was with me. She was driving. I had bought her a new sports car for her birthday—she had a thing for fast cars, and she had insisted that we take it to the party. I drove on the way there, to help go through the controls with her and give her some tips on how best to handle it. It was a powerful model that she had desired for ages. I'd had my doubts about buying it for her, but somehow I ended up doing just that.'

Unable to suppress the flash of guilt that jolted through him whenever he recalled Eliana pleading with him to let her have the car, knowing that he should not have allowed her to drive it until she had had more experience with it, Eduardo winced. There was a momentary ache behind his eyes.

'Anyway…when it was time for us to return home, she insisted I let her drive. Everything was fine until we were about ten minutes from our house.' Swallowing hard over what felt like dozens of tiny hot prickles layering his throat, he grimaced. 'There was a patch of oil on the road and the car spun out of control. I yelled at Eliana, to tell her what to do, and leaned across to help. But she was screaming in fright—her hands practically frozen on the steering wheel. It all happened so fast. We were on a mountain road and we hit a barrier at speed. She was killed outright. I lost consciousness. When I briefly woke up it was to find myself in the emergency room at the hospital, being prepared to be taken down to the operating theatre.'

'And after the operation—that's when they told you about your wife?'

'Yes.' Eduardo sighed.

With a distressed sound, Marianne laid her hand on his arm, gently stroking it over his skin, her eyes shimmering. 'It must have been awful for you to lose someone you loved very much so suddenly like that—and in such a terrible way.'

'Yes. There was a time when we were closer than close, but…'

'But what?'

'I—it doesn't matter right now. What matters right now is you and I, *namorada*. I am tired of dwelling on the past. Today is a new day, and I have enjoyed the most satisfactory of nights...in *more* ways than one. That being the case, I want to enjoy the day equally as satisfactorily.'

The glance he gave Marianne was full of meaning. But at that exact moment there was the sound of a car coming up the drive, followed by the front door closing.

'Ricardo,' Eduardo identified, tunnelling his fingers through his already sleep-dishevelled hair. He looked over at her ruefully. 'He must have returned from his trip. I will have to see him for a few moments.'

'Well, then...I'd better get back to my room and take a shower before I see to breakfast.'

'I will talk to Ricardo downstairs in the sitting room. Give me a couple of minutes, then you can leave—yes?'

'All right.'

Quickly dressing, Eduardo sensed Marianne's avid gaze on him. Briefly, and perhaps vainly, he wished that his body was as it had been before the accident...when he had taken much pride and pleasure in the supreme level of fitness he had achieved through running on the beach, swimming, surfing and working out in his own private gymnasium. *How did Marianne perceive him as he was now?* he wondered. Did she see a still vital and fit man in his prime, or did she see a man who had too easily succumbed to uninterest and despair about his future because of the physical ravages and mental agony suffered after his accident? Then he remembered what she had said about age and looks or any of that not being important—it was the *person* that mattered, none of the rest.

Eduardo wished no more interruptions were possible—either from distressing memories of the past or someone needing his attention. Because what he wanted more than anything else in the world right then was to spend the day alone with Marianne—to keep her preoccupied and tangled in his silken sheets, to make wild passionate love to her until, sated and sleepy, once again she fell asleep in his arms…

Glad that she had the distraction of several household tasks to occupy her, Marianne still had to try hard not to keep glancing at the time on her watch as she worked. In her heart she longed to keep the flame of the incredible intimacy she had shared last night with Eduardo burning, and she literally ached for his presence and for him to hold her again. But he and his valet had been ensconced in the sitting room for quite some time now, and only once during all that time had her lover come to find her, to request she make them some coffee. When she had taken the carafe to where they sat, along with two mugs and a plate of home-made shortbread, he had barely even glanced up to acknowledge her. She had slipped quietly out of the room again, oddly hurt that he seemed too preoccupied to give her so much as a smile.

But Marianne had every intention of holding true to the vow she'd made. *She wouldn't regret a thing*, she reminded herself. Even if she *did* become just another in a long line of women reaching back through the ages who had loved and lost the man they had given their heart to. She gasped softly as the idea crystallised in her mind. She didn't *love* Eduardo…she *couldn't*! She must be delirious or something. After her father had walked out and Donal had died she'd sworn to keep such a guard round her heart that no man would ever again penetrate it. In the matter of self-preservation she *must* and *would* adhere to that vow.

Just because she'd surrendered her virginity to Eduardo, it didn't mean that she loved him. Events were merely making her get a little carried away, that was all.

Seeking to drown out her troubled thoughts, she switched on the radio. Letting the mellifluous voice of the female presenter announcing the afternoon's programmes flow over her, she prayed that the upcoming offering of the play of the day—a gothic ghost story—would help distract her mind sufficiently to stop it from dwelling on one subject and one subject *only* as she worked…Eduardo.

Only seconds later, whilst examining the contents of the huge double-doored fridge to see what she could prepare for lunch, Marianne closed the door on her task, her thoughts ensnared by the remembered revelation that Eduardo had been married, and that his wife had been killed outright in the accident that had maimed him.

There had been something else he had almost shared with her about his wife, she recalled, frowning. There had *been a time* when they were closer than close, he had said… That suggested that they had been no longer close at the time of the accident. Why? Had the marriage hit difficulty? Had one of them perhaps had an affair?

What if it had been *Eduardo*? A wave of painful protest swept through her. He was such a vital, good-looking man. If his marriage had been on the rocks there surely would have been no dearth of interested women to console him?

Marianne groaned out loud, as if the sound itself could push the distressing thought away. For she could no longer fool herself about the truth… She had fallen as hard as it was possible to fall for this man, and if he was bereft of the ability to stay faithful then she couldn't possibly involve herself with him any further. In the past she had had a good friend whose husband had had an affair, and she had witnessed first-hand the destruction it had wreaked. Most of all the massive dent in self-esteem and personal worth that her friend had suffered, making her lose confidence in practically every area of her life and struggle to get through the day. Marianne had already experienced low self-worth and a lack of confidence, and she had no intention of revisiting either ever again…

'So this is where you are!'

At the sound of the man whose image had possessed her to the exclusion of all else that morning, Marianne turned. Dressed in a fresh blue linen shirt and jeans that snugly fitted his long muscular legs, with Cuban-heeled black boots, he was the kind of arresting sight that would wring a sigh of longing from any girl of sixteen to a woman of sixty and every age in between.

Almost overcome by her great yearning to be close

to him again Marianne leapt upon his inference that she must have been hiding—purely because she was feeling suddenly insecure.

'I think you'll find that I've been here the whole time you and Ricardo have been talking. Where else would I be, when there's lunch to prepare and dinner tonight too? I've already got up much later than I should have!'

'Do you think I want to make you a slave to the kitchen sink, *namorada*? Because, if you think I do, let me assure you that is certainly *not* my aim.'

Moving behind her as Marianne stood at the sink, where she'd been rinsing empty fruit cartons for the recycling bin, he slipped his arms round her waist and nuzzled her neck. The heat that shot through her made her feel like hot wax melting under a flame. It was all she could do to bite back the groan that threatened to leave her throat.

'However, I make no apology for having a hot little fantasy about seeing you standing here wearing nothing but an apron, perhaps a pair of high heels, and not much else!'

'Eduardo!'

'Yes?'

Turning in his arms to face him, Marianne steeled herself for the impact of his incredible blue eyes. It wasn't easy when she was already under siege from the intimate proximity of his body, as well as his admitted fantasy about her.

'Do you and Ricardo want something to eat? You've only had coffee and biscuits. You must both be hungry.'

Eduardo sighed, but not with exasperation. Instead the most beguiling enigmatic smile alighted on his well-shaped mouth and he impelled her closer, so that the heat from his denim-clad thighs seared into hers and Marianne's stomach was level with his lean hard hips. Feeling her defences frighteningly desert her, she stared up at him a little wild-eyed.

'You are always taking care of everybody else, little one,' he murmured, before bending his head and touching his lips provocatively to hers. 'What about allowing me to take care of *you* for a while, hmm?'

'What do you mean?'

'While he was away in London, Ricardo heard from his family in Rio. His mother is very ill and is in the hospital.'

'I'm so sorry.'

'Naturally he wants to go home to see her. As the severity of her illness is still unknown, and she has to undergo various tests, he will be staying there indefinitely. That means that you and I will be here together... alone. These past few days I have been feeling so much better having you around, Marianne... better than I ever could have believed possible. I think it will be good for us both to have the opportunity to get to know each other even more. Don't you?'

The days following Ricardo's departure for Rio would be etched on Marianne's memory for ever. She was no longer simply Eduardo's housekeeper but his lover, and to her utmost joy she had become his good friend too. The snow started to melt but the cold still bit hard—so they shared many conversations round the fire, talking about books, films, art, the state of the world—*everything*. It was a revelation to them both that they shared so many similar opinions. And when Marianne *did* differ from Eduardo she was not afraid to tell him so. She even gently mocked him sometimes for being old-fashioned, when it transpired that he wasn't the biggest fan of a lot of modern technology, believing it to be distracting and the benefits spurious, not to mention with the ability to suffocate imagination.

The closeness and companionship that had evolved between them—as well as the unforgettable nights they shared together in bed—helped her self-confidence soar—and, if Marianne was honest, her *hopes* for the future soared too.

One afternoon she was in the kitchen, preparing a special evening meal for them, with a good bottle of wine from Eduardo's selective cellar and candlelight, when she heard him enter the room behind her.

'Hi.' She smiled warmly, glancing up from the chopping board and wiping her eyes. 'Don't worry—I'm not crying. I've been peeling onions.'

Reaching her, Eduardo took the small vegetable knife out of her hand and laid it down on the worktop. 'Can we talk?' His thoughtful gaze made its usual intense reconnaissance of her features.

'Sure…what's up?'

'I have decided that I have had enough of the British winter and I greatly desire to go back to Brazil for a while. I plan to shut up the house and go in the next couple of days. To tell you the truth I have become quite homesick, Marianne.'

'So what are you saying?' Consumed suddenly by disappointment, and hurt at hearing this news, Marianne stared up at him in shock. 'That you want me to leave and find a job somewhere else?'

'Are you crazy? Just the opposite, in fact. I want you to return to Rio with me.'

'As what? A companion and housekeeper?'

It was not possible for Marianne to sort out the confusing profusion of feelings that seized her just then, but she knew that fear was predominant amongst them. Fear that the wonderful closeness developing between them would quickly take second place once he returned to his homeland, and to friends and family she didn't know but who had obviously known his wife.

Perturbed by her question, Eduardo frowned. 'As my *lover* and the woman I am having a relationship with,' he said firmly, drawing her into his arms. 'Is it not obvious that we have long gone past the employer/employee scenario?'

'And how am I to keep myself if I no longer have a job?'

'Do you really need to ask me that? *I* will look after you, Marianne. You will not have to worry about anything.'

Because Marianne suddenly felt cornered, she tried to

break out of his embrace. But Eduardo held her fast, apparently determined to get to the bottom of her disquiet.

'Would you not welcome the chance of some hot sun and a little pampering for a change, instead of all the difficulty and sadness you have endured?'

Feeling her eyes burn with the effort not to cry, Marianne sniffed. So used to managing on her own—at least until those six gentle months with her dying husband—she could sometimes be unraveled when someone expressed kindness or thoughtfulness towards her, as Eduardo was doing now. What would he say if he guessed that she wanted to be so much *more* than just an intimate companion to him?

Because her senses were suddenly raw, she went for attack instead of defence. 'Maybe it was wrong that we slept together. I came here because I needed a job and a home...not a holiday or someone to take care of me! Don't get me wrong—I'm totally happy for you to go back to Brazil and be where you belong again, Eduardo...amongst friends and perhaps other members of your family...but I really don't know if I can go with you.'

'No? What is it that is really holding you back Marianne? It is not as though you have any ties here to prevent you leaving, is it? You said yourself that you have not seen your father for years and do not even know where he is. And, although you insist that you still need a job and a home, we are in a relationship now. I have already told you that I want to take care of you, and you will not want for anything if you come back to Brazil with me!'

'For how long?' Her voice sounded as though it was about to break as she gazed back into those almost ethereal blue eyes.

The broad shoulders in the pristine blue shirt lifted in a shrug. 'How do any of us know how long our relationships will last, *namorada?* We enter into them in good faith at the beginning, but sometimes life takes too great a toll. Look at what happened to me, and then look at what happened to you. All we can do is take one day at a time…is that not so?'

Lifting her chin, Marianne saw Eduardo's glance was both wise *and* tender, and she found herself wondering how she could possibly spend even *one* more day with this incredible man without pledging her love to him for ever?

CHAPTER ELEVEN

AS SOON as Eduardo directed the Mercedes he'd picked up from the airport into busy rush-hour traffic heading into the city, the tension behind his eyes and in the pit of his belly increased. For over six months he had been cocooned deep in the English countryside, seeing no one but Ricardo, his doctor and his physio, and later—when he was able to walk with more ease—the odd shopkeeper when he walked into town. Other than that, until he had met Marianne, his dealings with other members of the human race had been minimal…just the way he wanted it to be.

Certainly the frenetic pace of life here had almost been relegated to a barely recalled memory…*almost*. Now, as the hot afternoon sun beamed through the windows, bringing him face to face with glaring reality, he was undeniably unsettled and, because of the circumstances that had made him seek refuge abroad, apprehensive too. The tension in him had already been heightened back at the airport, when he had been hiring the car. If he had thought to slip quietly back into Rio unnoticed then he had definitely deluded himself. The young man taking his details had knowingly narrowed his gaze at the mere sight of Eduardo, then proceeded to sorrowfully express his condolences on his wife's passing.

Eliana had been a well known soap star in Brazil, and inevitably her face and Eduardo's had been instantly recognisable wherever they went. Graciously thanking him for his kind words, Eduardo had known the man's obvious interest had aroused Marianne's curiosity, but he had chosen not to explain what all the fuss was about right then. *There would be time enough once they reached his beachfront house in Ipanema for him to tell her about his deceased wife's celebrity and consequently his own.* Yes, and to tell her that philanthropy had not been his *sole* occupation.

There were other things he wanted to share with her too…more personal revelations that should be revealed… But how? He had kept his thoughts about his marriage and the accident to himself for so long that they had turned into a debilitating and heavy suitcase that he permanently carried, and unhappily he had got used to the weight. Since it had begun to dawn on Eduardo that it was a terrible added burden on top of the tragedy itself, and that he might finally be free of if he shared it with Marianne, he had become determined to do exactly that.

But his main aim in returning home was to start picking up the threads of a life that had been deeply scarred, almost beyond bearing, and at last start to live again. Somehow…by some *miracle*…he had started to believe that he deserved that chance—and Marianne was a big part of that miracle. That was why he had chosen to return first to Ipanema, rather than his estate in the countryside. No more would he hide, or shut himself away from the rest of the world like some wounded hermit.

The other reason for coming to this livelier part of Rio was for his companion's benefit. For a girl so young and beautiful she too had had her share of tragedy, and he hoped that with a little luxurious living, pampering and sunshine she would blossom. Then slowly, given time, the memory of her husband's premature death and her distressing family life would fade. What Eduardo hoped most of all was that she would begin to see the benefits of being with him long-term and decide to stay. He knew it would sound unbelievably macho and possessive, should he speak the words out loud, but he honestly felt that Marianne *belonged* to him now—it was just plain unthinkable that she should live alone, or with someone else other than *him*.

Adjusting his dark sunglasses to fit better over the slight bump in the bridge of his nose, he grimaced as she sat quietly beside him in the passenger seat, staring out at the long line of traffic in front of them. She sighed.

'I am afraid it is always like this during rush-hour,' he told her. 'I should have timed our arrival better, but I'm afraid I took the first flight available. Do not mind all the waving of hands and passionate exchanges of words from the other drivers. It looks more dramatic than it really is. We Brazilians are a nation of soap-watchers—or telenovelas, as they are known here. We make no apology for enjoying a little drama in our lives! Some might call it life imitating art.'

'Are you all right?'

Her quietly voiced question cut through the nervous static in Eduardo's brain and acted like a lifeline. Becoming accustomed to Marianne's uncanny perception where his feelings were concerned, he should have known his enforced jollity would not fool her. Now, instead of dismissing her concern as he might well have done not so very long ago, he actually *welcomed* it. *But then the more time he spent with this intriguing and lovely young woman the more Eduardo found himself becoming infatuated with her.* He knew that he would not have returned to Brazil at this stage without her.

'Yes, I am fine.'

'You *can* talk to me, you know. You don't have to pretend you're feeling fine if you're not. I realise that returning home for you will have its challenges as well as its pleasures, and I want to help make things easier if I can.'

'You have already made it easier by coming with me. I am very glad that I was able to persuade you.'

'Like it was difficult!' She grinned. Her dazzling eyes were concealed behind her sunglasses but her pretty mouth—sweetly shaped and devoid of lipstick—lifted in a wry curve. 'To leave the British winter behind and fly out to Rio, where the sun is shining and the beaches are legendary? Even an unsophisticated girl like me wouldn't refuse *that* kind of persuasion!'

Eduardo stole a long, appreciative glance at her in the now near-stationary traffic. She wore a simple white sundress...the only summer dress she owned, she'd confessed...and although it was a loose non-figure-hugging style, like the Victorian nightgown she wore to bed, it was unbelievably sexy on Marianne's lithe slim figure, with her long hair flowing down her back.

Feeling his limbs pleasantly flood with languorous heat, Eduardo did not fight the surge of desire that gripped him—he simply enjoyed it. All last night, until they had risen in the early hours to leave for the airport, Marianne had stoked the fire in him to fever pitch—as she had on the many previous nights they'd been together—and he had barely been able to keep his hands off her. Now, as he gazed at her, seeing the sun turn the colours in her hair into a blaze of honey and gold, the fire that she aroused in him simmered again. Impatience flashed through him that they were still so far from the house, where he would at last be able to get her alone and have her to himself.

'I like it very much that you are unsophisticated, *namorada*. You have no idea of the power you have at your fingertips by that fact alone!'

'Power?' Behind the huge sunglasses that dwarfed her elfin face, Marianne frowned.

'Yes—power. A man would have to travel a long

way to find a woman as innocent and beautiful as you are, Marianne, and I mean that as a *compliment*. You have no idea how tired men can get of women who feel they have to behave like men to get on in life. It is completely refreshing to meet someone like you…someone who doesn't care about climbing some career ladder but instead is willing to follow her passions!'

'We're moving again,' she said softly, and Eduardo turned his attention back to the road and the now steadily moving traffic.

And if his heart leapt and his pulse quickened at the idea that they might get home sooner than he had first believed…then who could blame him?

Everything Marianne had heard was true. The beaches *were* spectacular. Long white bands hugging the coastline and shimmering in the blazing sun next to a jewel-like sea. And Eduardo's perfect modernist house, with its pristine white walls and ready access to Ipanema Beach, was the quintessential accompaniment to such spectacular appeal.

As he assisted her from the car, she gazed out at the horizon of white sand and glistening sun-kissed water, hardly able to believe that she'd made the switch from whiteness of a completely different kind—deep snow and frost that had at one point seemed it would stay for ever—to this…this *paradise* on earth.

A young maid and a male house-servant were waiting to help transport their luggage into the house, and Eduardo took Marianne's hand in his. His other hand grasped his cane, but he was leaning on it much more lightly than when they had first met, she noticed. He led her inside straight to a state-of-the-art kitchen and poured her a long glass of cool lemonade from the fridge. The bitter but delicious tang of exquisitely fresh lemon burst on her tongue as she took a few sips, making her immediately smile with pleasure.

'This is heavenly!'

Taking the glass out of her hands to set it on the marble worktop, Eduardo reached for her, an intense look in his riveting blue eyes.

'So are you. The most exquisite and desirable thing in the whole of this house is you, Marianne.'

His words filled her with warmth, making her feel beautiful and desired. But deep down Marianne wanted *more* than just to be wanted by him physically. If she was honest, that was why she had determinedly subdued her doubts and agreed to come to Brazil. It might be a wish that was fated not to be fulfilled, but she was hoping beyond hope that Eduardo might eventually discover there were other far deeper and more abiding reasons for him wanting to be with her than just desire. And if that were so then Marianne was willing to risk *everything* to be with him—even the possibility of him leaving her… like the rest of the men in her life had done.

His wife's tragic death might have forced him to flee his own country, leaving her haunting memory behind to heal his wounds far from the sunshine he was used to deep in the midst of a bleak British winter, but did that mean he could never contemplate another long-term relationship again, or even want to *try*?

'Hey,' he teased, his hands tightening a little on her waist. 'What are you thinking about in that mysterious mind of yours? I confess I am quite jealous that your thoughts seem to be elsewhere when I want them to be here, with *me*!'

'They *are* with you, Eduardo.' Reaching up on tiptoe, Marianne placed a small tender kiss at the side of his cheek. 'I was just wondering how you were feeling about being home again. This is such a lovely place I wonder how you could bear to leave it.'

'Sorrow and pain can visit paradise too, my angel.'

'Did you—did you and your wife stay here very often?'

As he considered the question, Eduardo's expression remained steady and tender—for once no visible shadow clouding the brilliant pale blue irises at the mention of his past. It lit a little flame of hope inside Marianne, and she breathed more easily.

'We tended to visit here separately…with friends or on our own,' he answered thoughtfully. 'In truth, we did not spend a lot of time together in the latter stages of our relationship, before she died.'

'Oh?'

'I can see that you are curious about that—but right now, before I try and satisfy any more questions, why don't you go upstairs to the bathroom and take a shower? I'm sure you would like to wash off the dust of our travels before I show you the beach and then drive to a nice bar that I know for a cocktail?'

'That sounds divine!'

'The shower?' Eduardo teased. 'Or the beach and the cocktail?'

'Both. But don't you want to take a shower too?

As he trailed his hand down her throat onto the pale smooth skin above her breasts, Marianne saw a tiny muscle flicker in the side of his cheek,

'Are you saying you want me to join you?' he asked, his voice lowering.

Recognising the hot flicker of desire that stole instantly into his eyes, Marianne felt her limbs turn deliciously weak and her head swam hotly—an occurrence that was becoming a habit whenever he gazed at her like that. No wonder the poets likened being in love to being afflicted by some kind of malady or fever!

'I didn't mean that.' Shyly dipping her head, she fiddled with her hair. 'But I'm—I'm not averse to the idea either.'

'That is what I love most about you, *namorada*,' Eduardo grinned. 'Your candour. You do not play games, like some women do. And now you have inadvertently put the idea into my head I find I cannot eject it—so come...we will go and shower together.'

As he led her to the foot of a modern spiral staircase that ascended to the upper floors through an opened door to her side Marianne glimpsed what she assumed must be the living room. A tasteful gallery of large framed photographic prints caught her attention. Even from a distance they looked sensational.

Following her riveted gaze, Eduardo stilled beside her.

'Can I look?' she asked, her mouth drying nervously in case he refused.

'Be my guest.' The broad shoulders lifted in a non-chalant shrug.

There were various stunning portraits of extraordinarily beautiful women—young *and* old—scenes that captured the colour and excitement of the country's famed *carnaval*, and nature photographs that suggested they might possibly have been taken deep inside the Amazon jungle. But, whatever the subject, each was executed in a way that made the viewer stare in wonder at its extraordinary beauty and the consummate skill and genius of the photographer.

'These are simply stunning, Eduardo.' As the words left Marianne's lips she recalled that day in the snowy English town when she had spied a look on his face that had definitely reacted to her comment about music being her passion. It had always made her wonder. Then she remembered the look of excited recognition from the young man arranging the car hire at the airport, and mused if there was a connection.

'*You* took these?'

'Yes…I took them,' he said, sighing softly. Eduardo's smile was not quite even. 'This is—*was* my passion'

'Was?' Her heart thudding—because she suddenly knew that the accident had cost him *much* more than she'd first believed—Marianne looked at him straight. 'If it's your passion, then how can you even think of giving it up?'

Jamming his hands into the back pockets of his jeans, Eduardo moved his head slowly from side to side. 'I was not in my right mind when I made that decision. I was hurting and angry and I did not feel that I deserved to do the thing I loved.'

'Because your wife died and you lived?'

He scraped his hand through his hair, and his expression was momentarily anguished. 'I should have been driving that night…not her. *I* was the better driver…the one who knew most about handling such a powerful car!'

'And how long are you going to go on blaming yourself for the accident, Eduardo—for the rest of your life? Did *you* spill oil on the road? These terrible things happen from time to time, and because we have no control over events we feel helpless and afraid, and we start believing we are the cause of them. We stop thinking clearly and drive ourselves crazy with "what-ifs". Well, in my opinion you've suffered enough. You've endured countless operations to mend your leg, and tortured yourself with guilt night after night since the accident happened. Now you've got to try and put the past behind you…make your life over again.'

'Like *you* have?'

'Like I'm trying to.' Suddenly self-conscious, Marianne knew her smile was a little awkward. 'We're *all* a work in progress.'

'You are right, as always, Marianne. Seeing this gallery again, I realise I cannot and do not want to give it up at all. *This* is what I came here to do...what makes me happy.'

'And it is your gift to the world, Eduardo. That's why you must never, ever think of giving it up again!'

Daring to take the initiative, Marianne moved closer to wrap her arms round his waist. The sensation was so heavenly that for a moment or two she laid her head against his chest, breathing in his warm, musky cologne and happily listening to the strong steady beat of his heart. It was on her lips to say *I love you...* But at the last minute the words stayed inside her throat unsaid, that old fear of being left or rejected keeping them prisoner.

'You know what I want to do now, don't you?' Kissing the top of her head, Eduardo folded his arms tightly around her, urging her closer.

Feeling his hardness strain against his jeans and press into her belly, Marianne curved her lips into a knowing little smile against the cool linen of his shirt. 'Take me to bed?'

'My favourite words.'

Eduardo's lips found hers and hungrily claimed them...

CHAPTER TWELVE

THEY were sitting outside on the terrace of a fashionable bar in one of the chic neighborhoods backing onto the beach. Some of the wealthier locals frequented it. On the small stage inside was a sultry female singer, backed by a colourful and enthusiastic samba band. Eduardo had told Marianne before they went in that the bar had been a regular haunt of his—a place where he would more than likely encounter friends and neighbours he'd known for years—and had asked if she minded that people might stop to say hello?

Seeing the mixture of concern and doubt in his eyes, Marianne had hastened to reassure him, sliding her hand into his and drawing nearer. Intimacy and love had made her bolder. Inside, a strong desire was growing to let Eduardo see that she would be a support to him for as long as he needed her. She hoped that that might just be *for ever*, but just knowing that he was at last open to being with people again—would not be shutting himself away through guilt and pain as he had done in

England—filled her heart with hope and gratitude for the change.

And, indeed, a steady stream of well-dressed people *did* stop by their table as they sat companionably listening to the music and sipping their cocktails. Each and every one of them greeted Eduardo as if he had returned from the dead—such was their pleasure and joy at seeing him. They were also extremely respectful towards Marianne—not one of them remotely regarding her as though she were a usurper.

When they finally had a moment to themselves, Marianne leaned across the octagonal wooden table, the gentle sound of samba music still playing in the background, and commented, 'All your friends are so glamorous! I feel like I've wandered onto the set of *High Society*—distinctly underdressed in comparison!' Glancing uncertainly down at the pale lime linen trousers she'd donned, along with a plain white gypsy-style blouse, she knew that although they were clean and freshly ironed they had definitely seen better days.

'Brazilians love to dress well—they believe you are what you appear to be, and that the world treats you better if you take pride in yourself.' Her handsome companion cupped her face, casting his tender gaze over every feature, not hiding his admiration. 'You have nothing to worry about, my angel... You are easily the most beautiful woman in the room...with or *without* clothes!'

'Eduardo...please!' She blushed hard, in case anyone had overheard, and didn't see the tall, statuesque blonde wearing a figure-hugging black skirt and blue satin low-necked blouse heading towards their table until she stood right in front of them.

'*Com licença*...Senhor De Souza...you probably don't remember me, but I'm a journalist working for a Rio newspaper on the arts page and I was a friend of your wife's. My name is Melissa Jordan...originally from New York. We met once at a party in Copacabana.'

Eduardo politely rose to his feet to shake her hand. For an instant Marianne thought she saw a flash of hot colour sweep his jaw—as though he were embarrassed. Whether because he had no memory of the woman or because she'd been a friend of his wife's she had no clue.

In the next second, Miss Jordan herself cleared up the confusion.

'You *don't* remember me, do you?'

Her tone was shrilly accusing, even *unbalanced* as she studied Eduardo.

Marianne felt a small shiver of distinct unease roll down her spine.

'Why should you?' the woman continued, swaying a little where she stood.

Had she had too much to drink? Worriedly, Marianne realised that she *had*. 'We hardly move in the same élite circles, do we? Thank God your wife wasn't a snob, like you! No wonder she'd had enough of being married to you... I heard she was pretty sick of your philandering too! Who's this?' The brittle ice-blue gaze of the blonde swung down to Marianne, who was still seated. 'Your latest little bedmate? How fortunate for you that your wife died when she did…it saved you having to pay a ton of alimony to keep her quiet about your antics, didn't it? We wouldn't want the newspapers printing a story about their best-loved photographer having a less than perfect marriage, now, would we?'

'I think you have said quite enough for one day, Miss Jordan, and now you had better leave. All you are doing is causing embarrassment to yourself, as well as spoiling other people's enjoyment of their evening.' Speaking quietly but firmly, Eduardo put his hand beneath the woman's elbow, as if to steer her in another direction, but she instantly shook it off and scowled at him.

'Leave me alone! I know your type…spoilt rich playboy who thinks he can treat women however the hell he likes! I can find my own way out, thank you very much!'

The blonde swayed and stumbled, and would have gone crashing to the ground if Eduardo hadn't steadied her just in time. By now some of the patrons at the other tables on the glamorous terrace, with the awesome sight of Sugar Loaf Mountain looming in the distance, had turned to see what all the commotion was about. Meantime, Marianne's body had gone from burning hot to icy cold at the vitriolic content of Melissa Jordan's horrible little speech.

Catching the barely discernible nod of Eduardo's head as he turned his gaze towards the part of the restaurant that was under cover, she wasn't surprised to see the smartly suited manager appear. With a murmured apology to Eduardo and Marianne *he* escorted the intoxicated journalist from the building.

As he returned to his seat, Marianne saw that the incident had definitely disturbed Eduardo, but he hid his discomfort well. It was only because she was coming to know his every little frown, nuance and guarded look so well that she knew he was shaken at all.

Leaning back in his chair, he took a moment to straighten the cuffs on his jacket and run his fingers round the rim of his shirt collar. His smile at her was brief as well as controlled, she saw.

'I truly regret that happened just then,' he remarked, his voice deliberately lowered. 'I hope it won't spoil our own evening.'

'*Did* you know her?' Marianne asked, secretly appalled at the doubt she heard in her own voice. But how could she help having doubts when the things the woman had said had struck right at the heart of her deepest insecurities, causing all kinds of havoc inside her?

'At first I thought not.' Sighing, Eduardo leant his arms on the table, casually linking his hands. 'But when she mentioned the party in Copacabana I realised that I *had* met her before, and on that occasion too she made a complete nuisance of herself.'

'So she *was* a friend of your wife's?'

'An acquaintance, that is all. Eliana did not particularly like her, as I recall. But occasionally at those parties and fundraising events we attended there were people on the periphery who saw them as an opportunity to somehow advance themselves. People like Melissa Jordan. She asked me to help her get a promotion by putting in a good word about her to the editor of the paper on which she worked—a man who is a personal friend of mine. I will help anyone who is genuinely in need, but her request was so blatant…*demanding,* even…that I am afraid I had to put her in her place and decline. She clearly still bears a grudge against me for that.'

'And the things she said alluding to—to you seeing other women when you were married?'

Marianne was suddenly feeling so distressed that her throat was threatening to close. Eduardo's calmly voiced explanation sounded both plausible and rational, but how did she know for sure he was telling her the truth? She loved him to distraction, but she wasn't naïve enough to believe that love couldn't make you blind to a lover's faults.

'You seriously think I would behave in such an abominable way?'

'I—I don't know…I mean, I…' Miserably Marianne hung her head, her heart pounding so hard that her chest hurt.

'Come!' Pushing to his feet Eduardo glared at her, then beckoned a nearby waiter, at the same time throwing some notes onto the table to cover their bill. 'We will go home. The evening has been ruined after all, and I really have no desire to stay here any longer.'

* * *

Standing on the balcony, listening to the Atlantic waves surge onto the distant shoreline then away again, Eduardo left the drink in his glass untouched as he stared out at the horizon. The sun had long gone down, and over and over again as he stood there in the moonlight he recounted that distasteful scene in the bar. Had Eliana *really* confided in the pushy journalist that night at the party, telling her that her marriage was in trouble? All it would have taken was an off-the-cuff unguarded comment and someone like Melissa Jordan, with her eye on the main chance and a talent for utilising her spite and making mischief, could have easily assumed that 'in trouble' meant Eduardo was seeing other women.

But even during their most trying times together he *never* would have cheated on his wife. Not even when Eliana had turned on him, threatening to have an affair because he had grown so cold towards her. Eduardo hadn't meant to be cold. He had just realised that his feelings were not the same any more…that they wanted different things, were pulling in different directions. How could they reconcile that? No, he concluded, Melissa Jordan had probably just made up that sordid little story about him 'philandering' because she was miffed at him for not succumbing to her pressure to help with promotion at work.

Bringing his mind firmly back to the present—far more crucial right then than what had happened in the past—Eduardo knew he was anxious to heal the disturbing rift that had so suddenly and shockingly opened between him and Marianne. He should have healed it straight away, on their return from the restaurant, but he had been so disappointed and angry that she would believe for even a moment that he was *any* of those despicable things the journalist had suggested he was that he hadn't trusted himself to be rational. So when she had declared she was tired and was going to bed he hadn't stopped her—even when he had seen by her pale, sorrowful face that she was distraught.

He *swore*…calling himself a not very complimentary name. Surveying his drink, he raised the glass to his lips, tipped back his head, and winced as the aged malt whisky hit the back of his throat and then swirled hotly into his stomach. She was too good for him, he thought miserably, resting the empty glass on the wrought-iron table behind him. He could not exactly blame her for believing the worst about him when from the start he had put up almost insurmountable barriers. It would serve him right if she walked out and never came back.

A spasm of profound anguish criss-crossed his chest and another violent expletive left his lips.

'It's such a beautiful night.'

Glancing up in shock, he saw Marianne standing in the patio doorway. She was wearing a knee-length white broderie-anglaise nightdress with delicate puffed sleeves. Her lovely hair was loose down her back and her feet were bare. Everything inside Eduardo tightened with almost unbearable longing at the sight of her.

'I didn't mean to disbelieve you back at the restaurant… You should know by now how much I care about you, or I wouldn't even be here.' Stepping out onto the balcony, she hugged her slender arms over her chest. 'But I do want to know about your marriage, Eduardo. How can I stay if there are secrets between us?'

'You are perfectly right.' His mouth compressed a little. 'There should be no secrets between us. The truth is that before she died Eliana and I had talked about divorce.'

Smoothing his hand over his mildly aching hip, but disregarding his walking cane, Eduardo moved a little closer to Marianne. The scent of Tipuana trees and the baked heat of the day floated on the air between them, even as the gentlest breeze lifted some strands of her hair.

'We had been married for ten years, and inevitably during that time we both changed quite a lot. My father had a coffee plantation, which I inherited when I was twenty-six and sold when I was twenty-seven. That was when Eliana and I got married. Managing the plantation didn't interest me, but photography did—so I pursued it as my career and was fortunate enough to make a name for myself. I had inherited a great deal of money from my father's estate, besides the money from selling the plantation, and I was making a very good living from my photography.

'Eliana had become a famous soap star, and she loved the good life…parties, fast cars, holidays abroad, *haute couture* clothes… To cut a long story short, she was becoming increasingly materialistic and ego-driven. Whilst I…' he paused to give Marianne a self-deprecating shrug

'…I was becoming more aware of my responsibility as custodian of the great wealth I had at my disposal, and more interested in discovering how best I could help those less fortunate than myself.

'Eliana grew unhappy at the amount of time I spent in that pursuit rather than attending tedious celebrity parties, or going on holiday after holiday, or accompanying her to the fashion hotspots of the world to see the catwalk shows that she loved… The tension and the rows between us worsened daily, until finally I could take no more. I asked her for a divorce and she agreed.'

Reaching the next part of his story—the part he had the heaviest regret about—Eduardo paused to rub his chest, feeling it tighten uncomfortably. He saw Marianne's gaze narrow with concern.

'Are you all right?' she asked.

'I am fine. I will finish telling you everything. I was at home one night at our estate in the country when she came back from a ball she'd attended—hosted by some aristo she'd met at a fashion show—and that night she was like the Eliana I'd known years back, when we first met. She was happy and—and suddenly affectionate towards me, and told me she wanted to talk about a reconciliation.'

Feeling himself colour, Eduardo nevertheless did not flinch from continuing.

'The inevitable happened. We spent the night together. But the following day when I was back at work I realised that I had not really wanted it to happen at all…that it had been a moment of weakness I was not proud of. I still wanted a divorce. I rang Eliana and told her the decision I had made. To my surprise she accepted it, telling me that she too thought it had been a mistake. The estate was vast enough for us to share residency without constantly bumping into each other, and so we agreed that was what we would do until the divorce came through.

'Just over a month and a half after that I remembered her birthday was coming up—our relationship had become much more amicable since we'd agreed to divorce—and I asked her what she would like as a gift. She reminded me there was a sports car she had been badgering me to buy her for a while. Some mutual friends were throwing her a birthday party and asked if I would come too…for old times sake. I agreed, and unfortunately that same night—that was when the accident occurred.

'There is something else I have to tell you…' He paused. 'When an autopsy was done on Eliana it was discovered that she was pregnant. Was the baby mine, or that aristo's? She'd once intimated she had been having an affair with him but I will never know.' Swallowing down his sadness, then sensing some of the tension in him disperse now that his story was almost over, Eduardo risked a smile. 'You know the rest…and now I have told you everything. Every word I have said is the truth…as God is my witness.'

'Eduardo?'

'Yes?'

'I have to ask you this. If your wife had lived and given birth to her baby…would you have stayed married to her?'

It was a question Eduardo had reflected on many, many times since the accident. And he would give an honest answer to this woman he now knew without a shadow of a doubt was the woman he loved with all his heart and could not bear to be without.

'No, Marianne…I would *not*. If the baby had been mine, he or she would have brought me nothing but joy, I am certain, but if it had been another man's he might have wanted to take responsibility, and Eliana might have wanted that. I always yearned to be a father, and I adore children. To have had my own son or daughter would have been—' he swallowed hard '—would have made everything else in my life pale into insignificance. But my marriage to the child's mother would definitely not have survived. We would have divorced, as we had planned, and come to some amicable arrangement about custody if the child had been mine. I am both positive and realistic about that.'

Marianne breathed out…slowly. Not a single doubt remained in her entire being that Eduardo had told her the truth. There was simply too much good in him for deceit. She only had to remember how he had reached out to *her*—some unknown girl singing on the street—and offered her a job and a home, even when he might have preferred to lose himself in pain and grief instead and ignore the rest of the human race.

'Thank you,' she told him quietly, her tongue briefly

moistening her lips. She furnished him with a smile. 'Thank you for telling me the truth.'

'There is something I need to ask *you* now,' he said.

'What is it?' At the grave expression on his face, Marianne's heart thumped.

'Did you love your husband very much?'

The question took her aback, but she wanted to give him an honest answer.

'He was a kind, good man—like you, Eduardo… And he was there for me at a time when I was desperate for a friend. So, yes…I *did* love him—but only as a friend…not as a woman truly loves a man. Not as I have come to love *you*.'

Now the man in front of her wore a look that was part joy, part disbelief, Seeing clearly that he didn't reject her, she felt hope and happiness surge into her heart.

'Say that again.'

And suddenly he was standing right in front of her, his light blue eyes transfixing her with their burning magnetism, his hands resting possessively at the sides of her waist, his breath skimming her face and making her skin tingle deliciously.

'I love you.'

'I can hardly believe it. But, seeing as you have just said the words to me, with a look in your eyes that tells me it must be true, I have no choice *but* to believe you! But how—how can you love me, Marianne? I am hardly a young woman's dream, with my bad temper and the way I can sometimes shut down and retreat into myself. I will probably drive you crazy when we are married, but I—'

Marianne's hands tightened against the biceps that flexed instantaneously and strongly at her touch. 'Married?'

'That is what I said. Will you marry me, Marianne? I certainly do not want you as my companion or my housekeeper for good! No…' His voice was filled with teasing warmth. 'Even though you could fill both those roles with ease I want you as my *wife*—my wife and the mother of my children.'

'I want that too, Eduardo, and it thrills me to hear you say it—but I can't help but think you're getting a poor bargain.'

'How so?' He frowned in concern.

'Well…I have no job, no money, hardly any possessions. I come from a dysfunctional family, and I'm not remotely interested in fashion, fast cars, or—'

'Or?' A dark blond eyebrow was raised in gently mocking amusement.

'Or football!' Marianne concluded, her teeth nibbling anxiously at her lip.

'Why football?'

'Need you ask? We're in *Brazil*, Eduardo! It's the nation's favourite game, isn't it? Even *I* know that!'

'Listen…if you ever say *even I* in that self-deprecating tone again—as if you're not an extremely bright, intelligent and perceptive woman—then I'll just have to spank you to knock some sense into you!'

'You wouldn't!'

'Want to try me?'

'Seriously, though… Maybe I used to talk about myself in a self-deprecating way…my mother leaving when I was fourteen, and my father being the way he was and eventually leaving too definitely had a bearing on my self-esteem… But back then I didn't really know who I was or what I was capable of. I didn't even know what I wanted in life. No…that's not totally true.'

Meeting his gaze with an unwavering stare, Marianne grimaced.

'All I've ever really wanted is to be loved, Eduardo. Yes…to be loved and not left alone by the people I give my heart to. But now I know that I have to think well of myself too—not keep blaming myself when things don't work out. I want you to know that I'm not looking for anyone to "complete" me any more. What I want is someone who'll be a true partner in life…someone who is there for me in good times and bad—as I will be there for *him*.' She grinned. 'Perhaps you're not getting such a bad bargain after all, now that I come to think of it!'

As he cupped his hands on either side of her face Eduardo's heart was in his eyes, and his glance lovingly swept over Marianne's animated features.

'All I know is that I am a lucky, *lucky* man to have found you, my angel. Trust me when I tell you I will do everything in my power to ensure you will not be left alone or unloved ever again, so long as I am with you.'

'I tell you what…' Drawing nearer, Marianne fingered the buttons on his shirtfront. 'If you ever hear me put myself down in the future…you could always try kissing me instead of spanking me.'

'You can be sure I will give your suggestion full and proper consideration, Miss Lockwood.'

Chuckling softly, then bending his head—his heart racing with joy—Eduardo kissed his lovely wife-to-be until even the stunning white sweep of Ipanema Beach and the powerful Atlantic Ocean ceased to exist…such was their complete fascination, devotion and love for each other…